DESIGNS ON YOU

DESIGNS ON
YOU
by carrie pack

interlude  press.

ISBN 13: 978-1-941530-04-7
Published by Interlude Press
http://interludepress.com

Book design by Lex Huffman
Cover Design by Buckeyegrrl Designs
Interior art photography: ©FreeImages/drniel
Cover art photography: ©depositphotos.com/gunnar3000
Cover Artist/Illustrator: Abby Hellstrom

For Granny—I like to think you'd have been scandalized and proud.

Chapter 1

"I'm dead, absolutely dead," Yvonne says, pulling her hands through her shoulder-length brown hair and throwing her arms up.

Scott looks up from his screen, where the pink and white stripes of a new logo design are burning into his brain, to find his art director looking frantic, her brown eyes wide with worry. He takes in her appearance. Messy hair, probably from the way she's been pulling at it; charcoal gray pencil skirt wrinkled and stretched out from frequent wear; her usually rosy complexion drawn and ashen. This, combined with the reluctant remnants of red lipstick around her mouth and a smudge of mascara below her left eye, makes her look positively frazzled. It's not like her.

"What's wrong?" he asks.

"My model for the One West campaign is about four inches too short," she says.

Confused, Scott furrows his brow. "Then why'd you hire him?"

He jumps when Yvonne slams a sheet of proofs on his desk.

"Well, just look at him," she says, pointing to one of the shots. "That jawline. That smirk. Boy's got face for days. He's perfect."

Scott looks at the images. They're small and a little dark from being run off their office's ancient laser printer, but she's right. His jawline is strong, but not too chiseled. His body is thin, but toned; he doesn't look starved like the models this designer usually books, but he's not as thick as a Calvin Klein underwear model either.

"How tall is he?" Scott asks.

"Five-ten, I think," she says. "Maybe five-eleven. Doesn't matter. Either way I'm dead."

"Can't you just use another model?" Scott knows they never shoot Jan West's line on just one model, especially not a featured piece. She's too important.

"The other guy who wore this suit has swollen collagen lips, Scott."

"Oh," he says, looking back at the proofs. The model really is stunning. He can't be older than nineteen or twenty, so he's probably still growing. However, Scott knows how particular Jan West is about using models who are at least six-foot-two. Her line is famous for its distinctive skinny-legged trousers, and she thinks the best way to create even more drama is to pick lithe models with extra long legs. This model has that in spades—and then some—but if he's only five-ten, they have serious problems. The One West line is their agency's bread and butter. If Yvonne screws this up, they could all be out of work.

"You want me to do some retouching?" he asks.

"Oh my God, could you?" Yvonne shrieks. "I would kiss your feet, Scott Parker."

He laughs. "No need for that. Anything to stop working on this stupid logo," he says, gesturing toward the pink-and-white monstrosity on his screen.

"Another cupcake shop?" she asks.

"Crème de la Cuppe," he says with a groan. "With two p's and an e."

Yvonne looks as if she's biting back a laugh, and Scott can't help but roll his eyes.

"I know, right?" he says. "It's like they're just mocking me now."

"I think Lorelei just likes to see your face when she gives you those projects," Yvonne muses. "Maybe if you hid your disdain better…"

"There is no hiding how I feel about logos for cupcake shops and vintage boutiques," Scott says. "It's just the way it is."

He sighs, thinking how he'd thought his career would have been further along at this point in his life. About to turn thirty and completely and utterly stuck in a deep, unrelenting rut, Scott can't help but remember that his aspirations had once included photography and sculpture, but he'd given it all up when he realized how difficult being a starving artist actually is. So he did what he swore he'd never do: took a job in graphic design.

"At least you've got eye candy to keep you company for a while this afternoon." Yvonne winks at Scott as she pats him on the back.

"I can't even tell you how happy I am that you screwed up so royally, Yvonne," he teases. "Thanks for brightening my day."

"Anything for you, Cupcake."

"I told you to stop calling me that."

"But it fits so well," she replies as she practically skips out of the room.

"See if I do you any more favors," he calls out after her.

Scott rolls his eyes and turns back to his computer. He opens Yvonne's file for One West and finds the most recent proofs. The files are all numbered and labeled "OneWest_Donovan_Fall13."

"Donovan." Scott says the last name out loud as he wonders what the model's first name is.

Scrolling to see which shots Yvonne has marked as possibilities, he opens one. It's a powerful image of the young model staring straight into the camera. His hands are in his pockets and his chin is tilted downward, lips drawn in a forced scowl, his jaw set—the tightness accentuating its strong line. The pose makes him look broader and older than he is, but the playful light in his eyes betrays his youth.

"You've got a mischievous streak in you, don't you, Mr. Donovan?" Scott says aloud as he opens the next photo.

It's a similar pose, but in this one the model is smirking. Scott smiles to himself. Definitely mischievous, he thinks. He wonders what the kid's story is. Where he's from. What his family is like. It's not like Scott to get so drawn into his work, but then again, retro logos and business cards aren't all that inspiring. This model, though—he's positively intriguing.

Scott muses whether he's from some elite East Coast family or a small, tight-knit Midwestern town—maybe California. Scott wonders if he was bullied growing up or if he had been a popular guy. Maybe he snuck under the radar the way Scott had.

Scott knows he was lucky. It could have been much worse, being gay and the artsy, chubby kid whose feet were too big for his body. He lost the weight, but somehow never has grown into his feet and trips over them so often it's as if his body needs to prove that he's still that same kid he was in high school. He wonders if his model had an awkward phase. From how he looks on the computer screen, it seems as if he always was this handsome, intense creature.

Scott isn't sure if he's jealous or proud.

As he sets to work on the images, tweaking them just enough to make the model look taller, Scott starts to develop a backstory for the young man in the photos. Only child, parents divorced. Was discovered in a mall in Minnesota his freshman year of college. He smiles to himself as he pictures the model in jeans and an ill-fitting T-shirt. It doesn't suit him. This man deserves to always wear designer clothing perfectly tailored to his stunning physique.

It's strange to be so curious about a person in a photograph, and yet Scott can't help but feel drawn to him in the way that a moth can't seem to resist a porch light on a hot summer night. In lieu of trailing off into more fantasies, Scott opts for doing his job.

He zooms in on the model's left thigh to make sure the muscle doesn't end up awkwardly shaped as he tweaks the image. It has to look realistic. As he inspects the way the fabric drapes over the model's leg, he admires the faint pinstripe; the trousers really are fantastic, well-fitted and flattering on the model's long legs. Scott really loves the One West line; it's definitely his style: classic but with a modern edge. But the pants never quite fit him because, with his stocky build and large feet, he's not built for the cigarette leg trousers. Still, he can appreciate the look.

"His legs are plenty long for these pants," Scott thinks. "I don't know what this woman's problem is. He's practically all legs."

And then his breath catches in his throat.

"Well maybe not *all* legs."

There, on full display between his legs and nearly life-size on Scott's monitor, is the faint outline of what can only be the model's cock. It doesn't seem to be even partially erect, but it's definitely not Scott's imagination. It's there. The bulge is distinct and now shockingly front and center on his twenty-seven-inch monitor. Scott swallows thickly as he tries to calm his breathing and remain professional. Fighting the urge to put his hand over the screen in case anyone walks by, Scott closes his eyes and takes a deep breath. He tells himself he's done this kind of work a million times; it's no big deal to have a model's crotch blown up life-size on his screen.

Opening his eyes, he considers the image on his screen with a more professional scrutiny. He'll definitely need to fix the bulge. The pants aren't very forgiving in that area—or maybe it's just this particular model.

He shifts in his chair as he scrolls just enough so that the model's crotch is no longer in the frame and he's focused solely on his thigh. He sets to work creating extra leg length and tries not to think about the other corrections he needs to make. He has to keep his focus for such precise work.

By the time Yvonne returns after lunch, Scott is just finishing the first photo.

"Nice work," she says, leaning over Scott's shoulder. "He looks great."

"Thanks," Scott says. "It's slow going, but I think we'll be okay."

Yvonne flops down in her desk chair and huffs out a harsh breath.

Scott turns to face her. "What?"

"So… Lorelei saw the test shots from the One West job and wants me to hire that model again," she says.

"That's good, right?" he asks. "She liked who you picked. The first time you chose the models, too."

"Right," she says running her hands through her thick bangs. "Except we have to doctor the photos… and more than usual."

"Oh."

"Yeah… oh," she says, leaning back in her chair to stare at the glaring fluorescent lights above her desk. "We're screwed."

"Maybe not," Scott says. "Now that we know what we need to do, no problem. You make him look as tall as possible at those shoots, and I'll work my magic here. Piece of cake."

"I don't know, Scott. That's a lot of extra work for you," she says. "And me."

"We'll manage," Scott says with a shrug. "Plus it's a really great opportunity for you. She's trusting you with a major client."

Yvonne smiles at him. "And you don't mind the eye candy either, right, Scott?"

"Well, I'm certainly not opposed to looking at an attractive male model for hours at a time."

Yvonne's smile grows wider and Scott can't help but grin back at her. "Have I told you how glad I am that I hired you?" she asks.

"Not since last Friday," he says.

By the end of the day, Scott has gotten through only two of the images Yvonne wants to use, so he saves the rest to his flash drive, planning to work on them over the weekend.

He doesn't get much work done, though, because he spends most of Friday evening telling his roommate, Ben, about the new One West model. The way his left eyebrow quirks up when he smiles. The few wayward hairs that make it look even more lifted as his perfectly crooked smirk tilts the opposite direction. The gleam in the soft green-gold hues of his eyes. The way the One West trousers hug snuggly to his lean, muscular thighs.

"You should see him," Scott says with a sigh. "He's perfection."

"So you've said," Ben says, not even trying to hide his eye roll. "Look, you know I'm supportive of your perverted fantasies and all, but I can only stand so much before I want to jab my ear drums with a pen. Can we just kill some zombies or something?"

Scott reaches up just in time to catch the controller Ben tosses at him, realizing how creepy he must sound, waxing poetic about the physique of a model he's never met. Ben has probably been humoring him since he got home; they've talked of nothing else.

Ben McComb, a lanky dirty-blond hipster with a fondness for pipe tobacco and craft beers, had answered Scott's ad for a roommate six years ago, and after a rocky start—Scott had erroneously assumed Ben was gay and had tried to set him up—they'd eventually become best friends. Ben was there for Scott through breakups and family drama, and Scott talked Ben off a ledge when he lost his entire savings trying to flip a condo just before the housing market tanked. They are more like brothers than friends now, so he lets himself get lost in the zombie apocalypse, keeping his thoughts of the new model to himself for the rest of the evening. But when Ben goes to the gym on Saturday afternoon, Scott opens the files on his laptop and stares at the model's profile.

He's hypnotized by the model's jawline and refined features. Scott has always loved this part of his job. Most male models have really great, chiseled jawlines. He's a sucker for a strong jaw. Something to nibble at.

His last boyfriend, Jacob, had a really great jawline. Scott had spent hours mapping it out with his tongue or just staring at Jacob in profile until it had earned him a grouchy "What?" and an eye roll when he'd replied, "Just admiring the view."

It still hurts to think of Jacob. Scott feels as if he failed somehow, maintaining the relationship for four years only to have it go down in spectacular flames when Jacob admitted he'd been fooling around for over a year.

Scott was devastated; he'd lost himself almost entirely—drinking in excess, sleeping with anything that moved and even losing his job as an art director at a prestigious agency—before Ben pulled him back from the brink. He's only just started to get his life back on track, settling in at Price Designs, even if it is an almost entry-level graphic design job. And Jacob still haunts him, because when they'd broken up, he'd lost not only his boyfriend but his best friend as well.

Scott misses the security of his relationship with Jacob—well, maybe he just misses that jawline… and possibly the blueberry pancakes he'd make on the weekends—but then he reminds himself that a jawline isn't the best foundation for a relationship.

Scott wonders if there's more to the model than his strong jaw and a devilish smirk. Not that it's *just* a strong jaw. After all, it's so perfectly paired with his slightly upturned nose, which can only be described as graceful, and his high, sharp cheekbones. Something about his profile is innocent and sexual at the same time, and it makes his entire face look like it's carved from marble.

Even his hair looks sculpted—high and brushed back from his face, it just begs to be touched. Scott imagines what it would be like to run his fingers through the man's hair, tugging on the thick strands as he bites at that jawline.

Scott has a fleeting thought that if he were still sculpting—as he had for a semester and a half in college—he'd want to create life-sized statues of this guy. He's just that stunning—his posture, his wide stance, his strong shoulders and tiny waist. If Scott could create a perfect specimen of a man from scratch, this would be it.

He forces himself to work on editing the pictures, though, getting slightly more accomplished than he had at work on Friday.

That night, Scott dreams of a stranger with a jaw made of sharpened razor blades. The man turns into a waitress who keeps asking him if he wants syrup on his pancakes. He wakes up in a cold sweat and heads straight to his closet, looking for the box of mementos he'd kept after the breakup. It's an over-sentimental mix of love notes and concert tickets, the few photos he'd bothered to print out, plus a ratty Chicago Cubs cap and a faux vintage Guns N' Roses T-shirt that both still smell faintly of Jacob's cologne.

Scott sits on his bedroom floor, dumping the contents of the box on the faded Berber carpet. He picks up a chocolate wrapper that had once been pressed flat and tacked up over Scott's desk at work. He turns it over in his hands and reads the words printed on the inside: *Don't be afraid to go after what you want.* Jacob had given it to him when he had toyed with the idea of starting his own graphic design business.

He dumps everything back into the box, pocketing the chocolate wrapper at the last minute, and carries it down to the dumpster behind his apartment. As he watches the remnants of his last serious relationship join a week's worth of smelly garbage, the Cubs hat landing in a puddle of sticky, brown goo, he smiles to himself.

Scott suddenly feels more free than he has in months and desperately in need of coffee.

"So I've made a decision," Scott says as he and Ben take a table at their favorite coffee shop.

"You're going to finally stop ordering that sludge and drink tea like I've been telling you to for years?"

"Funny," Scott says, taking a loud slurp of his black coffee for dramatic effect. "As if I'd give up the nectar of the gods for something as pretentious as Earl Grey."

"It's oolong," Ben scoffs, "and at least I won't die young from all the toxins in my body."

"You know, sometimes I wonder which of us is the gay man."

"Definitely you," Ben says. "We've talked about this. I could never suck dick."

The woman at the next table gives them a look of disgust before going back to her laptop. Without missing a beat, Ben discreetly flips her off and turns his attention back to Scott. "So what's this big decision?"

Scott leans back in his chair, preparing for Ben's mockery. "I'm going to try dating again," he says, grinning at his roommate.

Ben nearly does a spit take as he stifles laughter. "Yeah, right."

"I'm serious this time," Scott says, leaning forward. "I threw out the Jacob box. I'm ready."

Ben's eyebrows raise, his expression turning serious. "Whoa."

"Is that a good 'whoa' or a bad 'whoa'?"

"To be determined," Ben says. "But I'm proud of you. It's a step in the right direction. It has been over a year."

"Exactly. It's time. This is a new era," Scott says, sitting up straight and puffing out his chest. "Scott Parker is back on the market."

"God help the gay men of this city," Ben teases.

Scott kicks him under the table.

* * *

Despite his revelation and promise to start dating, Scott declines Ben's offer to be wingman at his favorite gay bar and spends Sunday evening at home. When Ben reluctantly leaves him sitting on their well-worn sofa, wearing his grungiest pair of sweatpants,

Scott settles in to finish the edits to the photos of the new One West model.

He opens the two images he hadn't finished Saturday, and his breath catches in his throat as he takes in the expression on the model's face. His lips are pulled into a slight pout, almost sulking like a petulant, angry child. His bottom lip looks plush and red and so ripe and…

Scott imagines how those lips would feel wrapped around his stiffening cock.

He almost chokes on his own air, looking around his empty living room as if there were someone around to catch him having dirty thoughts about a male model he's never even met. He blushes, even though he's alone. He feels guilty. This guy could have a family, a grandma named Mildred. A sister. A girlfriend… or a boyfriend perhaps?

He squints and looks into the man's eyes again, trying to keep his thoughts more professional. The model's expression reads a little bored in the shot, but his eyes tell a different story: seductive, teasing. He can see why Lorelei and Yvonne wanted to use him. It's hard to find someone with such expressive eyes.

Scott wonders what he looks like when he comes.

He quickly closes that image and tries to catch his breath. The room suddenly seems warmer. He tries to focus his thoughts on his work. He looks at the lone image left on his screen.

The last shot shows the model with his head thrown back and to the side, which makes his neck look impossibly long. The tendons are straining a little with the twist, and it's one of the sexiest things Scott has ever seen. He really wants to see this guy in person. Take him out to dinner. Bring him back to his apartment. Strip him naked. Hear him scream out his name.

Scott sets his laptop down on the couch and heads for the bathroom. He suddenly feels like a nice, long, cold shower.

He sits on the toilet lid for a bit, just listening to the water run. How did he get here? Treating his work like porn, fantasizing about someone he's never met. It's ridiculous and completely unprofessional. Maybe it's a good idea he's decided to start dating again, if for no other reason than he might actually have the chance to have sex with a real person instead of his own right hand.

* * *

Monday morning Scott rolls into work bleary-eyed and edgy from lack of sleep and too much self-inflicted sexual tension. He makes a beeline for the break room and is about to pour himself a cup of coffee when he sees Lorelei standing in the doorway, her black-rimmed, half-moon glasses perched low on her sharp nose.

"Scott, Yvonne is home with the flu. I'm going to need you to handle tomorrow's photo shoot. She'll email you our notes on styling and our test shots from the location."

"No problem, Lorelei," Scott says, beaming. "What account is it for?"

Lorelei is engrossed in something on her phone and doesn't look up. Scott pours his coffee into a chipped mug that reads, "I shot the serif," and waits for her to respond.

"Um… One West," she says, still looking at her phone. Her sleek, blonde bob falls forward, obscuring the expression on her face.

Scott swallows hard, almost dropping his mug. "Are you sure?"

"Is there a problem?" she asks, looking up at Scott over the rim of her glasses. Her gaze is piercing and her patience is obviously thin.

"No," he squeaks. Embarrassed, he clears his throat. "No. It's just a big account. Are you sure I'm the right—"

"It's our *biggest* account, Scott," she interrupts, tacking on a sigh. "And if we don't get those shots done tomorrow, we lose the location. I can't afford to wait for Yvonne to get over this plague she has. And everyone else is busy. So, yes, I'm sure you can handle it."

She's gone before Scott can eke out a reply. Stunned, he heads to his desk and sits down with a thud. He almost upends his coffee when his foot hits the side of his desk.

He should probably be worried about his first shot at directing a photo shoot at Price, but instead he's worried about meeting the new model.

How is he going to look this Donovan kid in the eye, knowing what he had fantasized about over the weekend? On the upside, he considers, he'll get to see this guy up close and in person. He's not sure if he wants to laugh or cry.

So instead he emails Yvonne.

From: sparker@price-designs.com
To: ytaylor@price-designs.com
Subject: :(

Yo-vinny,

I'm sorry to hear you're under the weather. Need some chicken soup? I open a mean can of Campbell's. (Stop giving me that look... I don't fit all the gay stereotypes. I like muscle cars, remember?)

So I'm sure you know, I'm covering the One West shoot for you tomorrow. Don't forget to send me your notes. I'm a little freaked, tbh.

Also, I may or may not have a bit of a crush on that male model. Haven't decided yet if this is the universe's way of mocking me or telling me to go for it.
-S

From: ytaylor@price-designs.com
To: sparker@price-designs.com
Subject: RE: :(

Notes are attached. You'll do great. Don't forget to tell Zach that he needs an extra strobe for tomorrow. The light in that loft is abysmal.

God, I feel like I got hit by a train. Soup won't help at this point. You think I could get them to put me into a medically induced coma for a few days?

Regarding your crush, the kid's kind of a dick, if that helps.

Gorgeous, but basically a total bitch. Swim at your own risk.
~Yvonne :)

* * *

In spite of Yvonne's scathing review of the model, whose first name Scott stupidly forgot to ask, he spends longer than usual getting ready for work the next day. He pulls out a black skinny tie he hasn't worn since college and a grey tweed vest he figures looks more fashion and less corporate because it's trimmed in black leather. True to his style, he dresses the look down with jeans, but the completed ensemble looks about as professional as he gets. He'd long ago given up on the business casual thing when he'd gotten his first tattoo. He decides to skip shaving and opts for his two-day stubble. He's always preferred the rugged look to the harsh burn of the razor anyway.

A quick glance in the bathroom mirror reveals that his unruly black hair is in its usual mood. He works some product through it to tame the frizz and wishes it would make up its mind—curly or straight. It's always been an unpredictable crap shoot. Some days his hair cooperates; some days it doesn't. Today it's the latter.

Scott takes one last look and double-checks to make sure he's not wearing anything recognizable from either a department store or a rival designer. Either one would get him mocked relentlessly by the stylist. Isaac is the kind of guy who pulls out your collar to check the label on your jacket. Scott figures vintage is safe.

He goes a little crazy on his cologne, probably because he's so jittery. Three cups of coffee will do that. He's likely to knock everyone out with the overpowering scent, but there's no time to fix it; he only hopes he can convince the cab driver to drive with the windows down.

He only fumbles twice with the lock. When he finally gets his key to slide in and turns the tumbler, he realizes he left his phone in the bedroom. He unlocks the door again and leaves his keys hanging in the lock as he retrieves it. By the time he hails a cab, he's running about ten minutes late and traffic is a nightmare.

Everything reeks of his cologne and he's starting to sweat. This day is so far a first-rate disaster.

Scott is so worked up by the time he pulls up to the location, he nearly throws his phone across the alley as he thumbs the lock screen while trying to read a text from Yvonne and pay the cab driver at the same time. For good measure, he shuts the car door on his hand. He sucks on his thumb, then shakes it out, trying to force the pain out through his fingertips. He looks down at his phone; his fingers begin to throb.

His name is Jamie, btw. ;)

Chapter 2

After wiping his hands on his jeans three times to dry his sweaty palms, Scott manages to pull himself together. He heads into the loft they're using for the photo shoot and sets out to find the stylist.

The heavy, metal door screeches loudly as he opens it, drawing the attention of several people he's never seen before. He offers an awkward, close-lipped smile, but they just return to their work, and Scott makes his way through the sparse loft that has become a flurry of lights, props,and clothing racks for the photo shoot. Early morning light streaming in from the windows to his left reveals a thick cloud of dust motes dancing in the air.

Scott makes his way through the commotion and finds the stylist crouched in front of one of the models. He takes in Isaac's appearance, his brown, wavy hair showing signs of thinning and shaved short on the sides and piled in a purposefully greasy mop on the top of his head, Scott barely recognizes him. But that's really not surprising. Every time Scott sees Isaac, it's as if he's completely reinvented himself.

As he approaches, Scott glances up at the model, who has his back to him, and he notices that Isaac is hemming the pair of grey trousers the model is wearing. Watching Isaac pull and tug at the crisp fabric, Scott's eyes are drawn up the model's long leg to the curve of his perfectly formed backside. It's the kind of ass worthy of passionate worship, given time and the right circumstances. Embarrassed by his momentary indulgence, Scott clears his throat, as if that might rid his head of inappropriate thoughts.

Isaac looks up at the sound and waves when he sees Scott. It's not just his hair that's changed; his face is much thinner and he's sporting at least a two-day beard.

The model turns his head to follow Isaac's gaze. And, of course… it's Jamie. Scott's intake of breath is so sharp that he has to cough to cover the sound. Jamie Donovan is even more beautiful in person.

Scott stares open-mouthed for a minute.

Jamie purses his lips and raises his eyebrows when he sees Scott standing there. He looks confused by Scott's presence, or perhaps annoyed at the blatant ogling. He looks down to Isaac, giving him the same questioning look.

"This is Scott Parker, our art director for the day," Isaac mumbles around the pins between his lips. He flips a strand of hair out of his face, but it immediately falls back to its original position.

Scott steps forward and smiles. "Yvonne's got the flu," he says, unable to think of anything else to say.

"I know," Isaac replies. "She fill you in on the concept?"

Scott nods. He needs to give him Yvonne's notes and try to get organized for the shoot, but instead, he walks around behind Isaac and takes in the full outfit: skinny-legged grey trousers and a jacket that looks like a cross between a leather bomber and a straightjacket. It looks amazing on Jamie.

"Hi," Scott says, extending his hand.

Jamie looks down at it as though it might burn him and slowly drags his eyes up to Scott's face.

"Charmed," he says with a lifted eyebrow. His voice isn't as deep as Scott expected, but it has a seductive, raspy quality.

Scott's eyes follow Jamie as he leans forward to look in the mirror, attempting to fix his already flawless hair. It's swooped up in an overdramatic pompadour that should look ridiculous, but Scott thinks it looks perfect, and he almost says so before he realizes he's still holding his hand out and Jamie has left him hanging.

Scott slowly withdraws his hand and shoves it into his pocket. "Likewise," he mumbles.

Yvonne wasn't kidding. This kid's an ice queen. It's kind of annoying. It's also kind of hot.

"Zach here yet?" Scott asks, forcing his gaze back to Isaac.

"I think he's setting up some lights over by the windows." Isaac jerks his head over his shoulder and Scott heads off in that direction.

"What did I do to get saddled with the newbie?" Jamie says just loud enough to be sure Scott hears it. "His cologne is toxic."

"Play nice," Isaac replies, not bothering to conceal his chuckle.

* * *

"Long time, no see, man," Zach says, greeting Scott with a firm, one-armed hug. "How's the desk jockey life been treating you?"

"Can't complain," Scott says. "They unchained me for the day at least."

Zach chuckles. "Should've gone freelance, man. We get all the best gigs."

"Maybe someday." Scott laughs nervously and glances over to Isaac and Jamie, wondering if he made as bad an impression as he imagines. The model and stylist are gone now, though, and he's forced to turn his attention to his work. He pulls his laptop out of his bag. "So, Yvonne emailed me her sketches. If you want me to show you, we can get started."

"Sure thing," Zach replies, grabbing his dreadlocked hair, pulling it back and securing it with a large elastic band. "Want to help me set up these soft boxes first?"

Scott tries to calm himself as he helps Zach finish setting up. He's known Zach for a while, so there's an easy camaraderie between them, despite Zach's imposing height and body-builder physique.

Things are really going quite smoothly, but between Scott's apprehension at directing his first shoot and the ire he'd drawn from Jamie, his nerves are frazzled.

By the time they call Jamie in for a few test shots, Scott's heart is racing and he's certain his hands are shaking—but he's afraid to look. He closes his eyes and takes a few calming breaths before Jamie appears. When he opens his eyes, he feels… not calm, but at least somewhat composed.

"Isaac, I think one of the pins came undone in the back," Jamie says as he enters Scott's periphery.

And just like that, Scott's heart starts beating out a rapid tempo again. He tries to discreetly wipe his hands on his jeans, but if the scornful look he gets from Jamie is any indication, he's unsuccessful in hiding this reaction.

Isaac hurries to fix the back of Jamie's jacket, a mess of clothes-pins and A-clamps keeping it snug to his body, while Jamie stands perfectly still. Scott is again reminded of a Greek statue. He's just so beautiful standing there in the warm, filtered sunlight, being poked and prodded as he waits patiently to be photographed.

Once Isaac is finished, he nods to Zach, who says he's sure he's finally got the lighting right. As Zach starts shooting rapid-fire, Jamie moves around so smoothly it's as if he's rehearsing an elaborate ballet. He's all long limbs and strong lines. Scott's breathing speeds up as he's overtaken by his own nerves. Feeling overwhelmed by the entire process, it occurs to him that he hasn't the slightest idea what he's doing as art director. And Jamie… well, Jamie is perfect.

Scott considers offering a comment or two when the angle doesn't seem quite right. He wants to say something about how Jamie's face would look better lit from the left side, but he's not sure if that's what Yvonne normally does. He'd been on photo shoots with his previous job, but only for home goods catalogs and that one taco chain that ditched his concept for a stereotyped Mexican in a poncho singing a jingle to the tune of "La Cucaracha." At those shoots, the "models" didn't really move much. It was set up a shot, take a few frames, move on. This is an entirely different animal. And there is Jamie, looking all gorgeous and judgmental.

Scott can't feel his feet.

"Scott, I'm going to start losing the natural light soon. Is any of this working?" Zach asks, dropping his camera to his side and glancing over his shoulder at Scott.

"You'd think an art director would *offer* his opinion," Jamie sniffs, lifting his head just a little higher.

Jamie's venom pulls Scott out of his daze. He clears his throat and gives Jamie a pointed look, suddenly spurred to action.

"Yes, that's good, Zach, but we need him to seem *taller*," Scott calls out. "Can we try it maybe from this angle?" He crouches down a little and mimes holding a camera. "Might make his legs look longer. And see if you can get more light on his left side."

Jamie's face falls a little before he forces it into a stony expression. "My legs are fine," he says. "Not that you'd know the difference, Gidget."

"Maybe it's the pose, then," Scott replies, standing up. "Could you try something less... I don't know... bitchy, perhaps?"

"Excuse me?" Jamie says. He no longer resembles a high-end model, but instead a belligerent teenager, the way he's looking down his nose at Scott. "If you'd just direct this shoot instead of worrying about my mood, we'd all be better off. If you wanted poses that make my legs look longer, all you had to do was fucking say so."

"Gentlemen!" Zach shouts, his booming voice echoing through the loft. "Let's focus, please. We only have this location for one day."

"Fine," Jamie huffs. His face relaxes and he falls effortlessly into a new pose. All signs of petulant child are instantly gone, the professional façade once again drawn over his features.

"Fine," Scott echoes.

If Scott didn't hate to lose an argument, he might compliment Jamie on the choice of pose. Because it *does* make his legs look longer, and, if it's possible, his face more striking. Combined with the angle Zach's shooting from, it just might work.

After that, the shoot goes more smoothly and Scott starts to find his footing, suggesting poses for Jamie and helping Zach move his lights while Isaac gets Jamie ready in the second outfit. Two other models show up after lunch— David and Noel—and Scott has better luck befriending them.

They chat about their hobbies—David, a muscular black man with a friendly smile, likes to play rugby, having lived in the United Kingdom until he was seven; Noel is the more quiet of the two and used to be a professional dancer, but he gave it up when he found modeling paid better. His mother is Arab, and he says he often gets booked for his "exotic" look, even though he's just a country boy from Alabama.

Jamie is mysterious as ever—Scott doesn't even know where he's from—and he sulks in a corner in between shots, eyes glued to his phone while he sips a Perrier. Scott shoots him sidelong glances periodically, wondering why he's so distant. Why would he want to be alone? The crew, the models, Scott—they all chat animatedly, laugh at each other's jokes and, in general, seem to get along. But Jamie hardly interacts with anyone. It makes Scott's heart ache in an odd way. He shrugs it off more than once. He's not even sure why he cares so much.

By the time they wrap at eight o'clock, Scott is feeling like an ass for blowing up at Jamie. Even if Jamie had been short with him, it was no excuse to bite back so harshly. It was unprofessional and really not like him at all.

He finds Jamie near the back of the loft, packing a leather messenger bag and looking even more stunning in his street clothes. David and Noel seem to be making plans for the weekend, but either Jamie is ignoring them, or they're ignoring him. David smiles at Scott and winks; he returns the smile and clears his throat.

Jamie looks up, his expression warm and inviting until he sees Scott standing near him, shuffling his feet nervously. When he makes eye contact with Scott, he sighs and rolls his eyes. Scott wonders for whom Jamie saves those friendly looks and finds himself really wishing it could be him.

"Look, I think we got off on the wrong foot…" Scott begins.

"Did we?" Jamie replies. "I think you pretty much put your foot *in* it." He doesn't look up from his bag and continues to pack up his belongings. When he finishes, he shrugs the bag over his shoulder and tugs a lived-in gray beanie over his auburn hair. "We done here?" he asks.

"Uh… yes?"

"Is that a question, or can I go?"

"Um, you can… you can go," Scott says, eyes wide.

"Wonderful." He gives Scott a tight-lipped smile and heads

for the door. "See you on Tuesday, Isaac," he calls out over his shoulder. And then he's gone.

Scott is left feeling raw and jittery—and something else he can't quite put his finger on.

The feeling stays with him through the following day, leaving him distracted and irritable at work. He's sitting in the break room, staring off into oblivion as he eats his lunch, when Lorelei drops her next bombshell.

"Zach sent us the proofs from yesterday's shoot. Yvonne's still out, so I'm going to need you to edit them down before the end of the day."

Scott swallows the bite of turkey sandwich he had been chewing and coughs a little as the still-too-big pieces catch in his throat.

"Is that a problem, Scott?" Lorelei asks. "I could always ask Marnie to do it, and you could finish that Crème de la Cuppe logo."

Scott shakes his head. "No, Lorelei. I'm on it. Really."

She smiles victoriously. "That's what I thought."

Scott turns to finish his lunch, just as she points her pen at him and adds, "Oh, and I need them before my four o'clock meeting with Jan West."

Scott hurries to finish his sandwich and heads back to his desk. He opens up the files with the previous day's date, and his desktop fills with thumbnails from the loft shoot. About two-thirds of them are Jamie. Scott didn't realize how much time they'd spent shooting with him. He remembers Zach really getting into a couple of poses and Isaac restyling one of the suits at least twice. But how had he managed to dominate the shoot with two other models there for half the day?

He throws out a couple of shots where Jamie's eyes are closed or where his hands are covering the belt and focuses on the rest.

It's obvious in his posture that Jamie really feels above everything when he's modeling. He is. But he's also a bit of a puzzle, because in some images he looks altogether different. The first five from the second restyle of the suit look softer, almost wistful.

Scott tries to remember what was going on when they took those shots. He had been talking to Zach about moving the chair in the background of the shot. And Isaac had been holding different ties up to the suit while he chatted with Jamie. Something about his family.

"How's your mom doing?" he asked.

"Better," Jamie said. "Still gets tired easily."

"A chink in your armor, Mr. Donovan," Scott says to himself, filing that away. Something to talk about maybe when, or if, he gets another chance.

In the next shot, Jamie is looking to his right. Just a quick glance, and it's only captured in one frame. What is he looking at? Scott racks his brain. He had been goofing off a bit, singing, dancing around, joking with Noel and David. Had Jamie seen them?

Something in Jamie's eyes for those few frames convinces Scott that there's more to Jamie than snark and disdain. Why is this gorgeous man so angry? Who or what has hurt him so deeply that he has no choice but to attack the world before it can attack him? Why is he so detached from everyone and everything?

Suddenly Scott is hit with an overwhelming urge to *know* Jamie. To truly understand him, know what makes him tick. Take him under his wing and teach him to laugh again. He looks as if he hasn't laughed in ages.

"He looks taller."

Scott starts when Lorelei appears over his shoulder. She leans toward his screen.

"Yeah," Scott replies. "I uh… had Zach try some new angles, and I told Jamie to try to elongate his legs as much as possible."

"Jamie?"

"The model." Scott points to the screen. "His name is Jamie." His face feels suddenly warm.

"I see," Lorelei says, tilting her head to look at Scott. She raises an eyebrow and then glances back at the screen. "Jan likes them to have long legs. Good thinking. I mean, this kid's got some nice stems, but he looks eight feet tall here. She's going to love it."

She pats his shoulder. Scott's shoulders relax as he turns back to his screen. Jamie really does look taller. The shots are good.

Scott smiles. "Thanks."

"Nice work, Scott. Maybe we should have you art direct more often."

She nods once and heads back to her office.

Scott gets back to editing the photos and wonders if Jamie's legs are as strong as they look. Is he a runner? Does he do yoga? Maybe both.

The more shots of Jamie that Scott edits, the more he's intrigued by him. Jamie's an undeniable enigma, and Scott really wants to break through his hardened exterior. If he ever sees him again, that is.

* * *

Yvonne returns to work on Monday, still slightly sniffly, but mostly back to her normal self.

"Sounds like you made an impression," she says, blowing over the top of her coffee mug.

"On...?"

"Lorelei," she says with a smirk. "I just came from her office and she wants me to take you with me on the One West shoot next week."

Scott turns in his chair to face Yvonne, eyes wide. "She what?"

"Yep, and I saw those shots, Scott. You fucking killed it. That Jamie kid looks even better than on the first shoot. Legs for *days*." She bites into her bagel and grins as she throws a sideways glance at Scott. "Not to mention, he looked hot in that suit."

"Stop."

"What?" she says blinking her eyes in fake innocence as she licks cream cheese from her bottom lip. "You don't think he looked hot?"

"That's beside the point," Scott replies. He turns back to his desk. "And anyway, you were right. He's a bitch."

"He definitely has an attitude. Did he do the eyebrow thing?"

"God... *yes*." He spins around in his chair.

"And it makes you want to slap him and kiss him at the same time doesn't it?"

"Kind of," Scott says. "What is that?"

"Models," Yvonne says, taking another sip of her coffee. "They're all the same. Hot as hell… and they know it."

"I don't think Jamie's like that," Scott says, feeling suddenly defensive.

"Oh?"

"Yeah." Scott twirls a pen on his desk. "There's something—I don't know… *different* about him."

"Oooh, does wittle Scotty have a crush?"

"Shut up," he says. "I don't know why I talk to you."

"Because we share an office," Yvonne says. "And I'm kind of your boss. You don't have a choice." She puts down her bagel and gives Scott a serious look. "This guy really got to you, huh?"

"No," Scott says.

"Uh-huh… sure."

"He didn't," Scott insists. "It's just… Okay, have you ever just had a feeling about someone? Like you just need to know more."

"Wow, you've got it bad, Romeo."

"It's not like that," Scott says, turning back to his screen. "I just feel like he needs a friend. He looks lonely." Scott tilts his head to one side.

"Then why is he working so hard to keep everyone at arm's length?"

Scott bites his lip. "Good question."

Chapter 3

That weekend, when Scott returns from a laughable date with a guy named Lewis—thirty-two, help desk administrator with six cats and a sweater-wearing Pomeranian—Ben greets him at the door with a beer in his hand and a suggestive grin on his face. Just as Scott finishes recounting his horrible evening—replete with details about Muffin's hairball problem—the first words out of Ben's mouth are, "So what about that Jamie guy? Have you asked him out yet?"

Scott's head falls back against the cool, brown leather of the sofa. "No, and I'm not going to, either."

"Why not? You wouldn't stop talking about him last weekend."

"It's not like that," Scott says, fiddling with the zipper on his jacket to avoid making eye contact. "I think he just needs a friend."

"A friend with benefits, maybe," Ben teases as he nudges Scott's knee with his own. "You were practically drooling on your laptop when I came home the other night. Don't tell me you wouldn't tap that."

"That's not the point."

"Care to clue me in, Scotty?"

"Look, I'm not in the market for hookups anymore, Ben. I want a real relationship, and Jamie clearly isn't into me. Besides, if I'm going to be his friend. I can't be his *boyfriend*."

Ben pauses, with a beer bottle halfway to his mouth. "What kind of dumbass rule is that?" he asks. "Something you read in Cosmo for Dudes?"

"You know how things turned out with Jacob," Scott says. "I can't do that again."

Scott and Jacob had met in college—they were both members of their campus' gay-straight alliance and became friends—but they hadn't dated until several years later when they got drunk at a house party and slept together. Scott had not yet learned to play his cards close to his chest and immediately asked Jacob out on a date. When they'd broken up four years later, Jacob had confessed he'd only wanted to get laid that night and Scott had been willing. Dating Scott had been easier than going out to find a new guy every night.

It was a hard-learned lesson, and Scott no longer expects to find love in a club, choosing instead to stick to one-night-stands when he needed them and keeping his close friendships separate.

"Okay, first of all, Jacob was an asshole. You can't judge every relationship by the horrible standard of that relationship."

"It's all I've got to go by."

"All the more reason to put yourself out there and see what happens," Ben insists before finishing off his beer and placing the empty bottle on the coffee table. "You're not getting any younger."

"Exactly," Scott says. "And Jamie's at least six years younger than me. I think it's better if we just keep things professional."

"Now you're just making excuses." Never one for deep conversation, Ben stands up and stretches. "I'm getting another beer. You want?"

"Sure, man." Scott stares at his hands knotted in his lap. Maybe Ben's right; maybe he is making excuses, but he's not sure Jamie is open to the idea of dating at all, let alone dating him. He'd barely spoken to Scott at the photo shoot, and when he did, he wasn't exactly friendly.

"I just don't think we'd be a right fit," Scott says loud enough for Ben to hear him in the kitchen. He hears the clink of bottle caps hitting the counter and knows he'll have to throw them away later because Ben won't. "Maybe I'm not his type."

"So shoot for friends and see where that goes," Ben says when he hands Scott a beer. "What have you got to lose?"

"Nothing, I guess," he says, ignoring the nagging feeling that there might be more on the line than he suspects.

* * *

"Whoa," Yvonne says when she picks him up Tuesday morning. "You look hot."

"Uh… thanks?" Scott says as he climbs into the SUV Yvonne rented for the day.

"No, really. I mean, you always look good, but this is more… relaxed. More you."

"So I'm not normally me?" Scott asks, scrunching his face in confusion.

"No, but this is *you*, you. Trust me. It's good." She turns her eyes to the road, but Scott can still see her smile.

"I just wanted to be comfortable," Scott says, looking down at his sweater and smoothing his hand over his jeans. "Last time I felt overdressed."

For his second photo shoot with Jamie—which is how he refers to it only in his own mind—Scott had decided to tone down his wardrobe a bit. He'd passed on the cologne entirely and picked a deep red cardigan to wear with a simple pair of jeans. Nothing special, and though he knows it looks good on him, he's really hoping it doesn't look like he's trying to impress anyone, least of all Jamie.

"Whatever you say, dear," Yvonne replies as she playfully pinches his cheek.

Scott ducks out of her reach. "Please don't act like this all day. I'd like to retain some semblance of professionalism."

"I'm always professional," she says, pulling her sunglasses over her eyes.

"Right," Scott says, buckling his seat belt. "Let's just go."

The photo shoot is for One West's holiday campaign and they're on location at an estate a few miles outside the city. A grand American colonial with four large white columns out front, it's one of those places that looks as though it would be perfect to live in, but in reality would probably be far more work than it's worth. There's so much open space that it would be impossible to decorate—at least not in a way that would feel homey or cozy—and it would never be clean unless you could afford to have a live-in housekeeping staff.

It is, however, perfect for a photo shoot, and it's decorated for the holidays with an ostentatious tree in the center of the grand foyer, even though it's only August and the heat outside is unbearable. Scott is regretting the sweater. It was fine in the air conditioning of his apartment and the car, but now, while he's helping Zach set up lights and moving decorations and furniture with Yvonne, he's starting to sweat.

"You could take the sweater off, you know," Yvonne says when she sees Scott pulling at the sleeves and fanning his face.

"I'm fine," Scott insists even as he feels a bead of sweat trickle down the back of his neck. He won't admit it, but he doesn't want to take it off until Jamie has a chance to see him in it. He knows it's nothing special, but schlepping around in a plain, white T-shirt definitely won't impress. And he *wants* Jamie to notice. He doesn't even stop to consider what that little desire might mean.

About twenty minutes later, the models still haven't arrived, and the room is stifling now that sunlight streams through the front windows. Scott caves and yanks his cardigan over his head, not bothering to unbutton it. His T-shirt comes with it and he has to pull it down to keep from completely disrobing.

He hears a choking cough and turns to see Jamie standing in the entryway, staring wide-eyed. They hold eye contact for a few tense moments, Jamie looking completely stunned as Scott tries to find his voice. He opens his mouth to speak, but Jamie beats him to it.

"Is this the kind of operation Price is running now?" Jamie says, rolling his eyes. "Can't even keep your shirt on?"

"Sorry?" Scott says. He shuffles his feet uncomfortably, wondering why everything comes out sounding like a question when he talks to Jamie.

"That's starting to be a theme," Jamie replies, lifting a paper coffee cup to his mouth.

Scott watches as Jamie swallows and licks his lips. He wonders how he is able to drink coffee in this heat without breaking a sweat.

He also considers that Jamie might actually look quite delicious gleaming with perspiration. Scott wipes the sweat from his own forehead in sympathy. At this point, he knows he's staring and he really should say something before Jamie thinks he's a total freak.

"Have you seen Isaac?" Jamie asks, sounding bored.

"He's, uh… in the first bedroom on the right," Scott says, pointing down the hallway to his left.

"Oh, so you *can* speak in complete sentences," Jamie says as he walks in the direction Scott pointed.

"Smooth," Yvonne says from behind him.

"Let's just get to work," Scott mumbles. He's annoyed with himself for not being able to charm Jamie. Although, right now he'd settle for not sticking his foot in his mouth every time he opens it to speak. Or at least not staring awkwardly as if he's never seen a good-looking man before.

* * *

Sadly, the awkward streak continues as the day wears on. Jamie looks even more gorgeous than Scott remembered. Scott has a hard time focusing on his work—dropping a vase and watching it shatter on the marble tile, stubbing his toe on a stray prop, knocking a full cup of coffee over onto a white linen tablecloth—so Yvonne has him go outside to set up the location for their group shots. The distraction helps Scott compose himself. A little.

And then, dressed in a thick shearling-lined coat and slim-fitted jeans, Jamie emerges from the house with the other models, chatting amiably with the same muscular model—David, Scott remembers—who had been friendly with Scott at the last shoot.

"Parker," David says, slapping him on the back. "I didn't know you were here. I saw Yvonne inside and figured you would be back to cupcake logos. You know Jamie, right?"

Scott nods, shocked that David remembers their conversation. He'd barely remembered David's name. With the mention of the cupcake logo, it occurs to him that maybe he complains about his job more than he realized.

"I don't think we've been properly introduced, though," Scott says, holding out a hand to Jamie. "I'm Scott."

"Jamie." He takes Scott's hand and pumps it once, dropping it as quickly as he can.

"You'll have to forgive Jamie," David says. "He's kind of a bitch, but I put up with him because he's got a hot roommate."

"She'd kick you in the balls if she heard you say that," Jamie says dryly.

"It would be almost be worth it," David says. "Have you seen her legs?"

"Gay, remember?" Jamie says, pointing at himself. "As is she."

"She's still hot."

Scott laughs but stops short when Jamie glares at him. He returns his attention to David.

"Actually," David says, leaning in conspiratorially. "Jamie only talks to me *because* I'm straight." He says it as though it's a shocking scandal that someone could be so mainstream.

Scott lifts an eyebrow and looks at Jamie.

"Jesus, David!" he says, swatting at his arm.

"Sorry," David says, but not sounding it at all. "Jamie here hates getting hit on, but I'm safe to talk to because I like girls."

Jamie is shooting daggers at David, but Scott refuses to give up.

"I can understand that," he says, giving Jamie his best friendly smile. When Jamie makes eye contact, though, Scott drops his head a little. He feels a blush creeping up his neck. "I bet you get hit on all the time. Probably gets old." He looks back up at Jamie and tries to smile.

"Wow… really?" Jamie says, tilting his head to the side.

Scott doesn't understand what he's said. He was agreeing with Jamie, complimenting him even. He looks at him with his mouth open.

"Typical," Jamie says and saunters off toward Isaac and Yvonne.

"What did I say?" Scott asks, gaping after Jamie.

"Dude, don't take it personally," David says. "Jamie's just like that sometimes. You'll get used to it."

Scott nods at David, who smiles before following Jamie to join the rest of the crew. Scott feels even more determined to break through Jamie's icy exterior. And maybe, he silently admits to himself, he's a little annoyed that Jamie seems to disapprove of *him* in particular. He wants to prove Jamie wrong.

* * *

Scott spends the rest of the day being extra attentive to Jamie: getting him water when he complains that he's dehydrated from all the sweating caused by wearing a winter coat in the heat; suggesting a break when he sees Jamie leaning heavily on a tree between shots; offering him sunscreen when he has to stand in the sun too long; laughing at his jokes when no one else does—anything he can think of to get in Jamie's good graces.

"I'm not interested," Jamie says as he takes the offered towel from Scott's hands on the last shot of the day.

"I'm sorry?" Scott asks.

"Whatever you're doing. All of… this," Jamie says gesturing with the towel toward the bottle of water in Scott's left hand. "It won't work."

"Just doing my job," Scott says, smiling.

"Your job is *not* to wait on me," Jamie says. "And I'm not interested."

"Oh," Scott says, eyes wide, and finally understanding what Jamie is getting at. "You think I'm hitting on you?"

"I don't *think*," Jamie says. "I know. And although it's sweet, I'm just not interested. I don't date people I work with. Sorry."

"Jamie," Scott says.

"I'm sorry," Jamie says. "The answer is no."

He gives Scott a stern look and is gone. Stunned, Scott can only watch him leave, his eyes landing on the way Jamie's thigh muscles flex beneath the unforgiving fit of the One West trousers. Scott can't understand why Jamie is so convinced he was coming on to him. He was just trying to be nice; that's hardly flirting. His behavior had been friendly but professional. Why is he failing so miserably at something so simple?

* * *

Scott spends more and more time thinking about that encounter with Jamie over the next few days, until it consumes most of his waking thoughts. Every time his mind wanders, he daydreams about Jamie. He thinks of the lift of Jamie's jaw whenever he looked at him, the disdain in his eyes, how gorgeous he looked angry. It should be really annoying. He should give up on befriending Jamie after he had been so damned difficult. But he just finds himself curious—about Jamie, about his past, his present… his life. If Scott were completely honest with himself, he might realize how attracted he is to Jamie, but instead, he drives himself to the point of distraction. It's so bad by Friday that Yvonne calls him out on it.

"I swear to God, Scott Parker, if you don't go out this weekend and have some fun, I'm going to fire your ass."

"Huh?" Scott says, prying his eyes from his screen where he'd been working on a logo for the last few hours.

"You've been off your game since that photo shoot. And I'm sorry that Jamie wasn't interested, but you need to get a grip," she says.

"I'm fine," Scott insists.

"You're using Papyrus, for crying out loud," Yvonne says, gesturing toward his screen. "You're NOT fine."

He turns back to his desk and stares at the mess he's created on his desktop. It's hideous. And he realizes he was daydreaming. He hadn't consciously chosen that font; he was just biding his time until he could get home and try to come up with ways to get Jamie to speak to him.

"I think I need a drink," Scott says.

"Or to get laid," Yvonne says under her breath.

"I heard that."

"Good," she says, reaching over him to close the file he has open. "Maybe you'll take my advice. Find a guy, have a few drinks, take him back to your place. You'll thank me."

She pulls his chair out and he lets her spin him in it until he's facing her.

"You know in some work places, this would be considered sexual harassment," Scott says.

"Go home," she says. "I'll see you Monday."

* * *

Scott heads home as Yvonne suggested, but he has no plans to go out and pick up guys. He just wants to lie around in sweatpants and order Chinese takeout, maybe play video games with Ben. He's too old for the bar scene these days. And besides, he still has photos to edit—photos of Jamie. The problem with that particular tactic is that Scott is forced to stare at Jamie's face—and body—for hours on end. Alone. In his apartment. On a Friday night.

It's not his fault that his mind wanders down a particularly pornographic path. It's probably less due to the way Jamie's ass looks in the pants he's wearing and more to do with the fact that Scott has gotten so familiar with his right hand lately that he should take it to dinner. He's just horny. Plain and simple.

When Ben comes home, Scott nearly falls off the couch trying to look casual.

"What are you doing?" Ben asks, smirking.

"Just, um… getting some work done," Scott says, "nothing major." He sets his laptop beside him on the couch and stands, tugging his shirt down self-consciously.

"On a Friday night? Didn't you *just* say you were going to get back out there, start dating again?"

"Um, well…"

Maybe Yvonne was right. Maybe he should go out, find some hot guy and get it out of his system.

"I was actually thinking about heading to this new bar one of the guys at work recommended," Scott says. "Wanna come?"

"Gay bar?"

Scott nods.

"No thanks, man. But you have fun." He nudges Scott in the ribs as he walks past. "Don't do anything I would do. You know, like girls."

"Your jokes are stale," Scott says.

"Just like your breath," Ben replies.

Scott rolls his eyes as he heads to his room to change.

The new bar, Cerulean, is overpriced and overcrowded, but there's a dance floor, and the guys aren't half bad, even if everything is lit in a ghostly shade of blue.

Scott heads straight to the bar in the back and orders a Jack and Coke, which is served to him in a bright blue glass featuring the club's logo. He takes a long, slow pull from his drink and turns to watch the mass of bodies on the dance floor. The crowd is just getting worked up and he can see a sheen of sweat on several of the guys closest to him. It's an average Friday night.

His eyes trail across a few of the men dancing with each other and he suddenly feels much too old to be there. These guys all seem to be barely old enough to have a fake ID. Scott considers just finishing his drink and going home.

And then he sees him.

Jamie, dancing by himself, although three guys are trying to get him to notice them, his eyes closed and his head thrown back as he bounces along to the beat, lost in the rhythm of the music. He looks like sex personified.

Scott puts his drink to his lips, rolls the liquid around in his mouth, and swallows hard. The whiskey burns its way down his throat as he watches Jamie lose himself in the sway of bodies around him. Jamie closes his eyes and dances with abandon, throwing his arms high above his head and tossing his head back. A tall, toned guy with washboard abs moves closer to Jamie so that their torsos are touching, and begins to match Jamie's movements. His deep brown skin makes Jamie's complexion look even lighter than usual, and the scene awakens a growling wave of jealousy in Scott's chest. He doesn't like the way this man is wrapping himself around Jamie, acting as if he's claimed his prize.

Jamie doesn't seem to notice, though. He closes his eyes again and lets the beat consume him, ignoring the man's advances.

The room is warm, and the beat of the music pulses through Scott's chest and vibrates deep in his belly. He watches as the man snakes a hand around Jamie's back and rests it just below his belt, his fingers teasing where the curve of Jamie's ass juts out from his lean waist.

Scott makes up his mind before he can chicken out. He downs the rest of his drink and slams the glass dramatically on the bar. Well, it *feels* dramatic, anyway. As he crosses the dance floor, he weaves his way through a dozen or so men who all seem to want to grab his ass, pull him in for a dance. But he doesn't stop. Not until he reaches his mark.

Scott taps Jamie on the shoulder, and he turns around and opens his eyes.

"Hey," Scott says, bracing for Jamie's usual venom.

"Oh my God, Scott!" Jamie yells over the music. "Dance with me!"

He grabs Scott's hand and twirls him on the spot. Scott can't help but laugh because Jamie is being so open and friendly. He looks young and free and damn near effervescent dancing like that. There's none of the previous disdain directed at Scott and it's wonderful. And Jamie's smiling. At him.

His previous dance partner seemingly forgotten, Jamie puts his hands on Scott's hips and guides his movements until he relaxes a little. At some point Scott manages to calm his nerves enough to sync his dancing with the pulse of the driving bass line. He lets himself get lost in the music and the simple feeling of Jamie pressed against him. And *God* does that feel good.

When the song changes to one with a slower beat, Jamie's arms find their way around Scott's neck, and he pulls him in tight to his torso. They're touching from chest to hip and their feet are tangled as they sway together.

Scott grabs Jamie's waist to keep from falling, the sensation making his skin feel warm and tingly at every point of contact. And even trapped in the midst of a sweaty, drunken mass of guys on the dance floor, Jamie smells amazing.

It's so different from staring at him on a screen. In pictures, he's stunning, a perfect specimen of what a model should be, but the reality of him is something else entirely. He's almost a different person, this mess of sweat and cotton with a hint of cologne wafting toward Scott's nose as he leans forward a little more and allows himself to get lost in the music.

By the third song, it becomes apparent that Jamie is more than a little drunk.

"I really hate you, you know," Jamie says into Scott's ear, slightly slurred, but loud enough so he can be heard above the music, and close enough that it sends shivers down Scott's spine.

"No you don't," Scott says, leaning in just as intimately.

Jamie pulls back, and his eyes are hooded and dark for a moment before he squares his shoulders and shakes his head slowly. It seems to clear the fog in his head.

"I need a drink," he declares and pulls Scott by the hand toward the bar.

Jamie orders two shots of tequila and smirks at Scott as he licks his hand to sprinkle it with salt.

"Bottoms up," Jamie says before licking the salt from his skin and chasing it with the shot. He scrunches up his face adorably as the alcohol burns its way down his throat. When he sucks on a lime wedge, he looks over at Scott, who is just setting his empty shot glass on the bar. "You need another drink," he says and waves the bartender over.

They do another shot, and Scott can't be sure if he imagines the way Jamie's tongue curls around the tip of his own finger, chasing a bit of lime juice. He orders another round, hoping Jamie will do it again.

After the third shot, Scott's head starts to feel more than a little fuzzy. Jamie shudders as he swallows and Scott laughs. Jamie sticks his tongue out playfully.

"So are you more of a *Mad Men* guy or a *Project Runway* groupie?"

"Huh?"

"Well, I mean you have the whole mysterious artist vibe about you, and you're art directing fashion shoots, but something about you seems very… I dunno. Corporate?"

"Wow, thanks," Scott says, sipping the drink he has in front of him, feeling the sting of Jamie's comment along with the whiskey; both feelings have a familiar burn.

"Not that you look stuffy or anything," Jamie says. "Not with these anyway." His finger traces the outline of one of Scott's tattoos, a traditional heart with a sword through it, emblazoned with his mother's name. The touch startles Scott, and he jerks away suddenly.

"No, I suppose the ink is a dead giveaway of my love for all things Heidi Klum," he teases.

"I just meant—" Jamie stops mid sentence and a huge grin breaks out over his face. "Oh my God, I love this song!" He grabs Scott's arm and tugs him back out onto the dance floor.

Before Scott can protest, they're dancing frantically to a remixed medley of punk songs, and he loses himself to the music. Jamie doesn't miss a beat as the music transitions from The Clash to The Ramones and then The Runaways.

"I can't believe you're into this," Scott shouts over the music. "You weren't even born when this music came out!"

"Neither were you!" Jamie shouts, not opening his eyes as he continues to dance to the music, his thick auburn hair bouncing in time with his flailing arms.

By the time they're sitting together in a tiny booth near the back of the club, sharing a bench and sipping mixed drinks, Scott has lost track of how many shots he and Jamie had at the bar or how many more drinks they ordered between trips to the dance floor. Scott doesn't quite know what's in his umbrella-adorned glass, but it tastes fruity and not really strong, which probably means it's extra dangerous.

He turns his head to smile at Jamie. This is the best night.

"Your hair is really awesome," he says.

"Oh, I bet it's a hot mess," Jamie replies, running his hand over the front of it where it swoops away from his forehead. It looks flawless in spite of all the dancing, the blue lighting making his red undertones appear purple.

Scott resists the urge to reach up to run his hands through it. "*My* hair is a mess," Scott says, rolling his eyes up as if he could see it for himself. "Too curly."

"I like the curls," Jamie says simply as he glances up. "Reminds me of a cocker spaniel we had when I was a kid."

"That's a funny word, cocker," Scott says, snorting out a laugh.

"You're drunk," Jamie replies.

"So are you."

"Maybe," Jamie says. He holds two fingers up and pinches them close together and closes one eye. "A little. I could go for some coffee right now. To sober me up."

"I love coffee," Scott says, chewing on his straw. "But I'm like the only person I know who orders black coffee at Starbucks. Like, I bet you're a soy latte kind of guy." He pulls the straw out of his mouth and points it at Jamie.

Jamie lifts his chin and stares down his nose at Scott. "Dirty chai tea, thank you very much."

"Still fancier than my order," Scott says with a shrug, dropping the straw in his glass.

Jamie smiles. It's warm and open and makes Scott's stomach twist in a wonderful way, or maybe that's the alcohol. Scott rests his chin in his hand and leans forward, smiling at Jamie.

"Have coffee with me sometime."

Jamie reels back, looking suddenly all-too sober for as much as they've had to drink. "What am I doing?" he says, trying to shove Scott out of the booth and climb over him all at once. "I've got to go."

Jamie stumbles a little, and Scott catches his forearm.

"Jamie… just wait. Jamie, what's wrong?"

He jerks his arm out of Scott's grip and loses his balance for a second before catching himself on the table. He stands up and tugs down on the front of his shirt, correcting his posture and standing tall again.

"I just need to go. I can't do this."

"Can't do what?" Scott asks. "We're just talking." He laughs nervously. Did he say something wrong?

"I'm sorry. I can't," Jamie says, looking completely horrified. "I have to go."

"Jamie…"

But he's gone, and Scott is left staring after him, trying to ignore the throbbing in his head from too much alcohol.

Or maybe it was from emotional whiplash.

* * *

Scott stumbles through his doorway—only dropping his keys once—just before two o'clock. He and Jamie had danced and talked for at least two hours before he'd run off. Scott's head still buzzes from the music and the alcohol, and he can still smell Jamie on his clothes.

He flops down on the sofa and nearly knocks his laptop to the floor. He catches it just as it's sliding off one of the cushions and flips it open. The photos of Jamie he'd been editing earlier are still open.

"God, you're sexy," Scott says out loud. He runs his hand loosely down the screen as if he could somehow touch Jamie's perfect skin through the cold plastic. It's not remotely the same, but Scott remembers the feeling of Jamie pressed against him on the dance floor and the way his eyes lit up when he first saw him. It was more than he could have hoped for when he'd first seen him across the club. But Jamie had been full of surprises.

"What are you hiding underneath all that fire and ice, Jamie Donovan?"

He scrolls through a few more photos until he finds the one he's looking for: an outtake where Jamie had laughed at David tripping over a prop. Jamie's eyes are nearly closed and his mouth is open wide enough to reveal a row of perfectly white teeth framed by his lush mouth and accented by the cutest dimples.

And it's so fucking sexy, seeing Jamie completely uninhibited just like he had been on the dance floor earlier, Scott thinks he might actually cry out of frustration. Instead, he unzips his jeans. He considers trying to do this without thinking of Jamie, but he's still a little drunk and too worked up to call on a different fantasy.

As he drags a hand up his torso, Scott wonders what Jamie's

hands would feel like under his shirt. Would he be rushed and heated or would he take his time worshipping Scott's body? His hand dips lower, underneath the waistband of his boxer briefs. Just a tease, but it sends a shot of arousal through his body like fire.

His mind wanders to the feeling of Jamie's breath, hot on his neck, when they had danced. The way his eyes had looked dark and seductive when they moved together. Surely Scott hadn't mistaken that look—arousal, attraction, desire. He's certain it was all there, even if Jamie didn't want to admit it.

Scott opens another photo from earlier in the day. Jamie is lounging on a retro-looking sofa. Scott doesn't remember this shot. It must have been one they did after Yvonne sent him outside. It's probably a good thing that she did, because Jamie looks positively sinful, his arm draped over the back of the sofa and his legs sprawled loosely in front of him, looking longer and leaner than before.

God, Scott wants those legs wrapped around him.

Jamie's head is turned to the side, face tilted away from the camera. The way he's seated on the sofa leaves just enough room for Scott to be able to sit down beside him and nibble his way up the long column of Jamie's neck while his hand grazes his perfectly soft inner thigh.

Scott arches into his own hand at the thought, and he almost upends his laptop. He grabs it with his left hand before it can slide off his legs. Scott readjusts and zooms in on Jamie's profile, not wanting to let go of the fantasy quite yet. He imagines the little whimpers Jamie would try to hold back as Scott teased his earlobe with the tip of his tongue. The way the tendons in his neck would shift and pull as Scott dragged his teeth over the sensitive flesh.

Scott trails his hand down his own neck and tries to imagine what he would say, what he would do, if Jamie would let him touch him like this.

"Jamie," he moans, taking his already hard cock in his hand. "Feels so good. God, I want you to touch me so bad."

He strokes down the length of his cock, keeping his eyes trained on the images of Jamie on his computer screen.

"You're so fucking gorgeous, Jamie. I want to map out your chest with my tongue, take you apart with my hands. Make you scream my name."

He's coming undone too quickly but he just doesn't care. He's picturing Jamie writhing beneath him as he takes him apart with each flick of his tongue.

"God, your tiny fucking waist," he says. "I could wrap my legs around you twice. Let you fuck me."

He slows his movements a bit as he rambles, wanting to draw this out, and his eyes fall on Jamie's perfectly styled hair.

"You're just begging for it, aren't you Jamie? To have that hair pulled? Messed up? To be owned."

Scott moans, and the thought of giving Jamie back some of his ferocity turns to toe-curling pleasure as his orgasm starts to build. He bucks up into his fist and feels himself begin to tip over the edge. His back arches and he surges forward as he comes, his entire body tensing before falling back against the sofa.

After a few moments, he opens his eyes and sees Jamie mocking him from his computer screen. At some point he had switched images and is now back to one of the earlier shots he'd been editing. The intense look he had found seductive now feels cold and judgmental. He rolls his eyes at himself as he reaches up to remove his stained shirt.

Just as he's lifting it over his head, he hears the unmistakable high-pitched giggle of one of Ben's drunken hookups echo through the hallway. He has just enough time to race to his bedroom, his jeans open, shirt bunched up around his neck, with his laptop gripped firmly in his clean hand, before he hears the key turn in the lock and the door slam.

Laughing at himself, Scott looks down at his computer screen where Jamie's image is still staring back at him, and he wonders what Jamie would think if he knew what Scott had just done. Guilt begins to creep in around the hazy edges of his booze-soaked mind, forcing him to face reality. Jamie had finally started to warm up to him, and he'd screwed it up, and then worse still, reverted to stupid fantasies and objectification by using Jamie's photos as his own personal porn. Dropping his laptop on the bed, he lets the spinning in his head overtake his body and lands face first on top of the covers, not even bothering to change his clothes.

When it becomes difficult to breathe, he rolls over, staring at the ceiling fan as it makes lazy circles above him. Did he really screw everything up by suggesting something as inane as coffee? Or is he that desperate to get laid that he can't even be friends with an attractive guy without wanting something more?

"You're just drunk, dumbass," he says out loud to himself. "Go to sleep."

He rolls onto his side, punching his pillow to fluff it. He can feel the room begin to settle, his drunkenness fading into unconsciousness. But just as he's dozing off, Ben's guest moans loudly. He tries to drown out the sound with his pillow, but she's apparently a screamer. Great.

His mind wanders to Jamie again, wondering if he's vocal in bed. Would he be the kind to talk, or moan or would he quietly revel in every moment?

"Oh, for fuck's sake!"

Frustrated with his inability to turn off his own brain, Scott grabs his headphones, hoping to drown out both the lewd sounds coming from the next room and his own rambling, perverted thoughts.

Chapter 4

While editing photos on Monday, Scott forces himself to think of Jamie in a strictly professional way—Scott is a graphic designer and Jamie is the model, period. He can handle looking at a handsome face and perfect body without fantasizing like a crude frat boy. And he can zoom in on his green-but-maybe-also-a-little-gold eyes and not get lost in the depths of them. A grown-ass man with a job to do can digitally remove creases from the fabric wrapped around Jamie's lean torso and long legs without imagining what he would look like naked. And twenty-nine-year-old Scott Parker can certainly keep from getting turned on while doing it.

He manages to stop himself from doing any of that, more or less, and to remain professional. Of course, that depends on how unprofessional it is to use his work as inspiration for his masturbatory fantasies. Because in the light of day and completely sober, Scott feels even more guilty about fantasizing so blatantly about Jamie; he tries to convince himself that his lack of romantic prospects lately had simply gotten the better of him, and his inner pervert had latched onto the first attractive guy he had seen. Jamie is simply an innocent bystander in Scott's decidedly lacking sex life. That's all.

But forcing his brain to think only the purest of thoughts about Jamie while he's safely ensconced in his work in the starkly lit confines of his office doesn't make it feel any less awkward to be facing him in person the following week at yet another photo shoot.

And it also doesn't help that just to prove to Ben that he can, Scott resolves to double his efforts at befriending Jamie. *Just* befriending. That means he has to face him and talk to him and probably get shot down yet again. But he doesn't care, because he seriously wants to get to know Jamie. Despite the awkward fantasies and the stilted conversations and Jamie's cold shoulder and all the careful posturing he's doing to keep Scott at arm's length, Scott still wants to know more. It's worrisome the way he's been obsessing over it, making up stories in his head about who Jamie is and where he came from. How did he get into modeling? What does his family think? Does he have a best friend, someone he can truly confide in? Does he have someone to love? A lover?

Scott wants to know all this and more, so on his way to the photo shoot, he buys Jamie a large dirty chai as a peace offering, adding a cappuccino for Yvonne when he thinks about her tendency to read way too much into his actions. As is the norm in Scott's imperfect life, neither gesture works out the way he planned.

"You brought him coffee?" Yvonne says as she takes her cup from Scott. "You must have really lost your mind this time, Parker."

"I'm just doing something nice for a friend," Scott says. "Not everyone has ulterior motives, Yvonne."

"True, but everyone needs to get some. And he's hot." She winks at Scott, which earns her another eye roll. There's no point in trying to convince her. She's made up her mind that Scott is just trying to get in Jamie's pants.

But Scott only wants to see Jamie smile again.

Scott's always been a sucker for a great smile. The first time he and Jacob broke up, after a huge argument, that's what had gotten him back in Scott's good graces. Jacob flashed his thousand-watt smile, and Scott forgot what they had argued over. He knows a cute smile is his weakness, but he can't help himself. He loves making people smile.

When they arrive on set, Scott finds Jamie in hair and makeup, his fair skin and thick, soft auburn hair almost daring the woman working on him to improve its perfection. Scott still can't believe how stunning Jamie is. It practically takes his breath away.

The makeup artist points a slender finger up and to the left, and Jamie tilts his face to follow her gesture. The movement causes the sunlight streaming through the open window to fall directly on Jamie's face, and it paints him with a breathtaking ethereal glow. The makeup artist dusts his nose and forehead with a soft powder, but she doesn't do much else, tilting his head left and then right to study his flawless complexion.

"Damn, boy, I'd kill for your skin," she says.

Jamie smiles at her. "Or I could give you the number for my aesthetician," he says, scrunching up his face. "Slightly less criminal."

Scott looks from one to the other. Her skin looks just as smooth as Jamie's, albeit much darker and offset by her blue-black afro. The bright clink of the bangles on her toned arm echoes Jamie's laughter as she swats at his arm playfully. Their easy banter makes Scott realize they must have worked together before.

"Sheena," someone calls from the other corner of the room. "Do we have any more of that spray foundation? I can't find it."

"I'll be right back," she says to Jamie.

He nods and pulls out his phone, immediately scowling at whatever is on the screen.

Scott, sensing he may not get a better opportunity to talk to Jamie alone, walks confidently toward him, smiling as if nothing had gone amiss the other night. When Jamie sees him approaching, he almost breaks into a smile before adopting his usual cool, aloof expression. Scott takes the brief hint of forgetfulness as a good sign, as Jamie looks questioningly at the two cups of coffee in Scott's hands.

"I figured if you won't go to the coffee, I'll bring the coffee to you," Scott says, presenting the paper cup with a flourish and a small bow. "And I wanted to apologize."

Jamie lifts an eyebrow, but he takes the cup from Scott's hand. He sniffs it before bringing it to his lips and taking a tentative sip.

"Dirty chai," he says with a hint of a smile.

"Well, I'd like to say I have great intuition, but it's more like a good memory. You told me the other night."

Jamie scowls a little, and Scott shifts on his feet and clears his throat nervously.

"Look, Jamie, I don't know what I did to upset you, but I want you to know that my intentions are completely pure. I just want us to be friends. I promise."

"*Just* friends?" Jamie asks. "Not friends with benefits or fuck buddies… but just friends?"

"Absolutely," Scott replies. Hoping to convince them both, he even holds up three fingers. "Scout's honor."

"God, you're a fucking dork," Jamie says, rolling his eyes. He looks as if he's about to say something else, but he pulls up to his full posture when he sees the makeup artist approaching, and asks, "We done here, Sheena?"

She nods at him and smiles at Scott.

Jamie stands up and unbelts his robe. As he turns, Scott feels his heart thudding loudly in his chest because Jamie is almost completely naked except for the tiniest pair of black briefs Scott has ever seen. He swallows hard and quickly tries to avert his eyes.

"Um, I should… I should go and find Yvonne," he stammers.

Scott trips over the chair Jamie had been sitting in and it crashes to the floor, taking Scott and his coffee with it. As he untangles his limbs, he rights the chair and smooths the front of his shirt, thankful it isn't stained. Even though his coffee is now a lost cause, he picks up the paper cup and puts the lid back on.

"I'll uh… I'll get someone to clean that up," he says, gesturing toward the spill.

"I've got it," Sheena trills, bending over and swiping the floor with a towel she pulls from her back pocket.

"Thanks," he mutters.

Sheena gives him a sympathetic look as she finishes wiping up the spill.

Scott needs to get away from Jamie before he makes an even bigger ass of himself. He hears muffled laughter as he retreats to the sparsely decorated set and the sanctuary of his work.

"Holy hell, Scott, what happened to you?" Yvonne asks when a flushed, sweaty Scott appears at her side. He's still holding his empty coffee cup and wondering where all the damned trash cans are.

"Nothing," he says, wiping his forehead with the back of his hand. "Let's just get to work."

Yvonne's gaze falls over Scott's shoulder and her jaw drops.

"Oh I see what's got you so worked up," she says softly. "Jesus, that kid is hot. It's not fair."

Scott turns to see Jamie, who has removed his robe entirely, leaning on the doorframe he'd just come through. Still sipping from the coffee Scott had brought him, he's back to giving Scott his usual icy glare.

Scott's eyes drag slowly up Jamie's lean body. He doesn't mean to, not really, but there's just so much to look at. He's sure he can see Yvonne's slack-jawed expression in his peripheral vision, but he's not ready to look away from Jamie just yet.

His muscles are obviously toned, but not so defined as to be considered bulky. He has a dancer's build, maybe from yoga or even swimming, Scott thinks. His skin is fair all over, and the way he's glowing in the morning light, Scott thinks he probably waxed for the shoot. He wonders briefly what their limbs would look like entangled—Jamie's fair, practically hairless skin against his own deeper coloring and dark, thick chest hair—but when Scott's eyes land on Jamie's arms, he finds tightly formed biceps that thus far have been hidden from view. They flex as Jamie lifts the coffee cup to his lips and swallows.

"Wow," he says, unable to stop the word from escaping his lips.

"Get an eyeful?" Jamie asks.

Scott blinks heavily as his brains slowly catches up to Jamie's words. The comment unfortunately brings his mind back to that night he'd jerked off to pictures of Jamie, his fantasies running rampant as he'd memorized the model's chiseled features, and he feels his face flush with shame, even as he remembers that Jamie can't read his thoughts.

"Um... what?"

"Like what you see?" Jamie says, enunciating every word like Scott might not understand him otherwise.

"Um... yes?"

Jamie snorts. "*Friends... right.*"

The disgust on his face shoots through Scott like an arrow; he wants to kick himself, or at least apologize for staring like a maniac, but Jamie turns abruptly and walks away, leaving Scott to gape after him.

"Whoa," Yvonne says, her mouth just as wide in disbelief as Scott's.

"Um, Yvonne?" Scott says, once Jamie is out of sight.

"Yeah?"

"Why didn't you tell me we were shooting underwear today?"

She gives him a tight smile. "Surprise?" she says, looking not the least bit remorseful.

* * *

After that, the entire day is tense, to say the least, but Scott manages to compose himself and not kill Yvonne. He keeps trying to make eye contact with Jamie, mostly because if he looks anywhere else he might spontaneously combust. He wants to talk to him, try to apologize, but when Scott offers him a bottle of water between setups, Jamie makes a point of asking Isaac to bring him a towel. When Scott suggests another pose, Jamie asks Zach if it looks okay.

The constant rebuffs are maddening and only spur Scott to try harder, his smile growing wider every time he looks at Jamie. Yvonne draws him out of a daze by elbowing him in the ribs so often, he's pretty sure there will be bruises later. But it doesn't matter, because he's a man on a mission.

None of it works, though. Jamie keeps his distance, and Scott becomes more and more crazed for his attention. Everyone on set becomes more awkward and exhausted from dealing with the tension, and the day drags on. When Jamie is changing in the back room that doubles as a dressing room, Scott hears muffled shouting coming from behind the closed door. It sounds like Isaac and Jamie, but he can't be sure.

When the fighting dies down, Jamie emerges, fuming, red-faced and breathing heavily. Isaac follows moments later, a triumphant grin on his face. Jamie's in the final look for the day—a slim-fitted sport coat over a simple T-shirt and dark jeans. He looks as if he's going on a date, and for some reason Scott finds that hotter than seeing him in his underwear.

Isaac tugs at the back of the jacket and Jamie wheels around.

"It's fine," he says, eyes flashing in anger.

Isaac gives him a pointed look with raised eyebrows.

"Fine," Jamie says, biting his lip.

Scott thinks he hears a quiet "thank you" from Isaac, but then Jamie is walking in his direction. He's absolutely sexy when he's angry.

"Have Sheena fix your makeup first," Isaac calls after him. "You're smudged."

Jamie purses his lips, looking like he wants to yell at Isaac again, but he just takes in a deep breath and heads for hair and makeup.

Isaac returns to help set up the final shot. Scott looks at him questioningly, but Isaac just shrugs and says, "Let's get to work. We're almost done, and I'd like to have dinner before nine at least one night this week."

Scott lets it go, and they get through the final shot without incident, even though Jamie still looks out of sorts.

Scott is flat-out exhausted and he just wants to go home. He's packing up his laptop and wondering if he should feel guilty for ordering pizza for dinner two nights in a row, when he hears an uncharacteristically timid voice behind him.

"Hey."

"Hey," he says in reply, noting that Jamie's still in wardrobe from the shoot. "Uh … Isaac will be right back."

"No… I mean. Well…" Jamie clasps his hands together and nervously cracks his knuckles by pulling on his own fingers. "I wasn't looking for Isaac. I wanted to talk to you. To apologize."

Scott blinks at him.

"For earlier," Jamie clarifies. "I was kind of a jerk."

"Kind of?"

"Okay, I was a total douchebag," Jamie says, dropping his head a little and laughing. "You have no idea what this is like for me."

"Modeling?"

Jamie nods. "And being completely objectified all the time. Sometimes I feel like I'm just a body—a face first and a person second. No one cares what I have to say as long as I show up on time and look good and…wow, I sound like a pretentious asshole."

"I think *I'm* the asshole," he says, smiling sheepishly. "I was totally ogling you. No wonder you think I'm a creep."

"I don't think you're a creep."

Jamie smiles, and the moment seems like flipping a switch—suddenly something has changed. Staring into Jamie's green eyes feels so intimate that Scott momentarily forgets all about his earlier indiscretions with the photos. It's an all-too-brief moment of reprieve before the embarrassment over what he'd done the other night comes rushing in. Scott feels his face grow warm and clears his throat. "So, um, if you feel that way about modeling, why do you do it?"

"Money," Jamie says quickly, and after a beat, "and it's not like I'm qualified for anything else—at least not anything that you can get discovered for in a mall while you're still in high school."

"You were really discovered in a mall?"

Jamie rolls his eyes. "I'm a walking cliché, I know."

Scott bites his tongue to keep from laughing at the accuracy of his guess about Jamie's past. "What about college?"

"College wasn't really an option," Jamie says, not offering to elaborate.

Something in his eyes looks wistful, or maybe defeated. Scott doesn't like seeing him looking so forlorn.

"Well, you're an amazing model, Jamie, but you shouldn't give up on education if that's your dream," Scott says, reaching out to place a reassuring hand on his arm. But when Jamie looks uncomfortable, Scott changes the subject. "And you don't look *that* young."

"I'm nineteen." He shrugs. "Anyway, modeling pays the bills better than working at Starbucks. And way better than being unemployed. Not to mention, I make a lot of connections."

"So why the ice queen routine, then?" He winces as soon as the words are out of his mouth. "Sorry. I didn't mean—"

"No, it's okay," Jamie says. He pauses and looks down at his hands, and for a moment, Scott thinks he might not answer the question at all. Jamie takes a deep breath and sighs, but he doesn't make eye contact as he speaks. "I just… don't like to date industry people." It comes out rushed and mumbled, but Scott just barely makes out his words.

He senses that Jamie's not giving him the whole story, but he doesn't push. "Well, I just want to be your friend. Swear."

"So you said."

"I meant it," Scott says. "Really."

"And it has nothing to do with the way you were ogling me earlier?" Jamie looks skeptical and something else. Hopeful maybe?

"Okay… fair point," Scott says. "You got me there." He pauses and steps closer. "Jamie, you're gorgeous; you know that, but that's not why I'd like to get to know you. And I mean the *real* you. Not the bitchy persona you've crafted to keep people at arm's length. And it has nothing to do with your body. I promise."

It might have a little something to do with your eyes, though, he thinks.

Jamie's jaw drops a little. Scott might have hit on something there, a window, opened just a crack, a tiny fissure in his façade.

"Besides, I think I'm a little old for you," Scott says, ducking his head and glancing up at Jamie, hoping he can lighten the mood.

"Maybe a little," Jamie teases. "But what are you, like twenty-five?"

"Almost thirty," Scott replies with a self-deprecating chuckle.

"So you're twenty-nine."

"Which is almost thirty."

"Well, we'd better start looking for a nursing home, then."

Scott laughs. He likes this Jamie—reminiscent of the Jamie from the club, but without the murky haze of alcohol to dull his own senses. Jamie is funny and smart, with just an edge of sarcasm, and yet there's something soft about him too, something kind and sweet. Maybe it's his youth, even though he certainly *acts* older than nineteen.

Scott's mouth falls open.

"Wait… you're only nineteen? But we had all those shots at the club…"

"Fake ID," Jamie says laughing. "Or didn't they have those in the dark ages?"

"Funny," Scott says.

They're silent for a moment. And it's not uncomfortable. Smiling, Scott holds Jamie's gaze for a few seconds, savoring the genuine smile he gets in return. For the first time since they met, it seems, Jamie isn't pushing him away, and it feels good. Promising. And for reasons Scott can't quite explain, life-changing.

"So… friends?" Scott holds out a hand for Jamie to shake.

"Friends," Jamie says, smiling wider as he takes Scott's outstretched hand.

* * *

Scott wakes up sweaty and panting that night in a way that hasn't happened to him in years. A vision flashes in his mind of what he'd been dreaming: strong, graceful, long legs wrapped around his torso and pale, milky skin set off by the tiniest black briefs. A soft, lilting voice speaking Scott's name like a prayer as they both came. A sweep of auburn hair falling over a flushed face while striking eyes pleaded for more. A man, a stunning, perfect man with eyes like galaxies and a personality that ignited Scott's imagination like wildfire.

Jamie.

He'd been dreaming about Jamie.

His head drops heavily on the pillow beneath him.

'This is insane," he says into the darkness. "You're supposed to be his friend. Not fantasizing about him in your sleep."

Of course part of him knows he's only trying to convince himself. Jamie is easily one of the most beautiful men Scott has ever seen, and certainly the most beautiful man he's ever been *just* friends with.

He shifts uncomfortably and kicks the sheets free from where they're tangled between his legs, only now noticing the sticky mess between his overheated skin and his boxer briefs. Scott groans and drags a hand over his face before forcing himself out of the comfort of his bed and into the harsh, fluorescent light of his tiny bathroom.

He throws his underwear in the hamper and turns on the shower as hot as he can stand. When he steps under the spray, the water pounds into his back and relaxes the tension in his muscles. He spreads his palms on the cool tile in front of him and watches the water swirl down the drain beneath his feet.

There has to be another way to deal with his attraction to Jamie. This is getting ridiculous: having wet dreams like a fucking kid; acting like a bumbling idiot whenever he sees Jamie; hiding erections from his coworkers as he edits photos. It needs to stop.

When Jamie had offered to exchange phone numbers, Scott had simply handed him his phone and nodded, even though he'd wanted to dance around the room from the joy trying to burst from his chest.

He hadn't expected Jamie would want to meet for coffee.

"I owe you, right?" he'd said. "For this morning." And then he'd smiled.

As Jamie had walked to the back room to change out of his clothes, Scott had clutched his phone to his chest like a lifeline, the words "call me" still ringing in his ears. Jamie wanted him to call. Part of him was secretly hoping Jamie would make the first move; Scott needed to know that Jamie was also invested in trying to be friends.

But it had been two days since the shoot and there hadn't been a phone call or text or anything. His phone had mocked him, cold and dark for the last thirty-six hours except for the stray text from Ben or an email from work. Nothing at all from Jamie.

Scott doesn't realize how long he's been in the shower until the water starts to run cold. He shuts it off and grabs a clean towel.

He's not sure he wants to call Jamie. The truth is, he's afraid. Afraid of himself. Of what he might do. Of what Jamie might say. Oddly enough, he's not really afraid of being rejected. If he's being honest with himself, Scott's more worried that this could be *something*. Something he's not entirely sure he's ready for. Certainly something Jamie isn't ready for. And that scares the shit out of him.

* * *

Three more days pass before Scott gets up enough courage to contact Jamie. It's a Wednesday, and he's editing photos from the last shoot. He's actually getting quite a bit done while trying to distract himself from the phone number burning a hole in his contacts list. Funny how it's a bit difficult to do that when he's staring at Jamie half naked in twenty-seven inches of high-resolution glory.

He pulls out his phone and rolls it around in his hand. One text won't hurt. Something work-related. He can do this; they're friends now. Jamie offered his number first. Said they should get coffee. It's fine.

He starts typing the message: *You should see these proofs from the shoot the other day. You look…* and here he pauses, unable to think of what to say. He types out "fucking amazing!" but that doesn't feel right. He deletes it and replaces it with "hot!" That still feels like too much of a come on. He deletes it again and types "like a Greek statue." Groaning in frustration at his own inability to not sound like a cheesy pick-up line, he deletes those words, too.

"Having trouble, Cupcake?" Yvonne asks.

"No," Scott lies. "Just some family stuff. Nothing major."

"Jamie looks great," she says offhandedly, gesturing to Scott's screen. "Lorelei's gonna love it."

"Thanks," Scott says as he glances down at his phone, the blinking cursor mocking him. He takes a deep breath and types out a single word—*great*—and hits send before he has a chance to second-guess himself for a fourth time, and, of course, he immediately regrets it.

What a dumb way to start a conversation. Couldn't he have said something safer, like, "Nice weather we're having," or, "Read any good books lately?"

Yvonne's attention is back on her work, so Scott has nothing to distract him from the fact that Jamie doesn't reply right away. Scott begins to wonder if Jamie is going to respond at all, and he thinks maybe he should have just said hi rather than mention Jamie's appearance. It's not as if he doesn't know better. Jamie had all but told him he didn't like getting hit on, and there he goes sending texts that sound like bad pick-up lines. Not to mention, he's ten years older than Jamie. Now he's just that creepy older guy who wants to be "friends."

Scott is so wrapped up in mentally flogging himself that when his phone finally buzzes with a new text message, he practically jumps out of his seat.

Yvonne gives him a sidelong glance as she walks past him on her way out of their office, but she doesn't say anything. When she's gone, Scott glances at his phone and smiles when he sees the message is from Jamie: *Slow day at work? You've got to have better things to do than stare at photos of me all day.*

Scott laughs because that's actually his favorite part of the day. Not that he'd tell that to Jamie.

He replies: *Well there weren't any urgent cupcake logos that needed designing, so I thought I'd go poke the polar bear.*

Jamie: *Not sure if that's a joke on my complexion or my icy demeanor, but I'll give you points for creativity.*

Scott: *So we're keeping score now?*

Jamie: *Yes, and I'm winning.*

Scott: *Guess I need to up my game then.*

Jamie: *This is me rolling my eyes at you. Don't you have work to do?*

Scott: *Just editing photos of this bitchy model. ;)*

Jamie: *Maybe he's not bitchy... maybe it's the dorky art director that's the problem.*

Scott: *You misspelled charming.*

Jamie: *You misspelled delusional.*

Scott: *Perhaps. I should probably get back to work actually. See you on Friday at the shoot?*

Jamie: *That's what they're paying me for.*

Scott: *Bitchy.*

Jamie: *You misspelled charming.*

Scott smiles at his phone. He can't believe he's actually becoming friends with Jamie and, compared with his first few attempts, it actually feels easy.

"What are you grinning about?" Yvonne asks as she makes her way to her desk.

"Nothing, just a funny text from a friend."

She shakes her head and smiles at him.

"What?"

"I have news," she says, her smile transforming to a Cheshire cat grin. "But if you're too busy…" She sits down in her chair and pretends to have lost interest in their conversation.

"Oh, come off it, Yvonne," Scott pleads. "Just tell me."

"It's really nothing," she teases, shuffling through some papers on her desk. She checks her lipstick in the mirror she keeps above her monitor. "So, next shoot," she says, without looking at Scott. "Lorelei wants you to run it."

"By myself?" he asks, setting his phone down on the desk.

Yvonne looks up and smiles at him. "Yep."

Scott's eyebrows squeeze together. "Why?"

"Well, these shoots don't need *two* art directors, Scott."

"She's promoting me?" Scott asks with wide eyes.

"Congratulations, Cupcake." Yvonne's smile widens at Scott's obvious excitement.

"Oh my God," he says, beaming. "I'm too excited to get mad at you for calling me 'Cupcake' twice in one day."

* * *

Ben demands that they celebrate, dubbing an evening of pizza and video games "Upgrade Night."

"Pizza got here fast," Scott remarks.

"Upgraaaaade!"

Scott opens a couple of beers.

"Upgraaaaade!"

Ben gets a better weapon than Scott in their video game.

"Upgraaaaade!"

It's irritating, but Scott is perfectly content to have a night in and celebrate something good finally happening to him. Buzzed and smiling, he reclines against the front of the couch, stretching his cramped legs. He wriggles his toes and arches his back.

"I can't believe I'm going to be in charge of that entire photo shoot," he says.

"Upgraaaaade!"

Scott chucks a pillow at Ben and misses his head by mere inches, nearly taking out a lamp that teeters precariously before righting itself, the lampshade creating a strobe effect as it swings over the bulb.

"Okay, okay… I'm done," Ben promises, holding up his hands in mock surrender as he tries to contain his laughter.

"Thanks, man… for all this, I mean." Scott gestures around their living room, which is now littered with pizza boxes, Ben's dirty socks, every video game they own and several empty beer bottles. "I really needed a night like this."

Ben reaches for his last slice of pizza. "Don't go getting all mushy on me," he mumbles through a mouthful of half-chewed cheese and pepperoni.

"Civilize yourself, dude."

"Not a chance," Ben replies, opening his mouth wide to give Scott a better view.

Scott rolls his eyes. "I need new friends," he says.

"Good luck with that."

"With what, new friends?"

"Yeah… like that Jamie kid." Ben gives him a skeptical look. "You can't even get him to talk to you."

"I'll have you know I've made a lot of progress in that area," Scott says. "I even got his phone number."

"That sounds more like a booty call to me." Ben punctuates his sentence with an exaggerated eyebrow waggle.

"You do realize two gay dudes can be friends without it being sexual, right?"

"Not when one of them finds the other hot." Ben's smile is smug and Scott has the urge to smack him.

"I'm over it," Scott insists. "We're friends. Just friends."

"Uh huh. Sure."

This time the pillow hits the lamp, which crashes to the floor, shattering the bulb.

Chapter 5

Friday morning is one of those glorious late-summer days that's sunny and warm, a reprieve from the oppressive heat as the season eases toward fall. Scott is beyond grateful for it because they're shooting outside all day and there's no way he could stand the kind of stifling humidity they've been subjected to for the last two weeks. Fall is coming, and Scott just wants to enjoy the last bit of summer while he can—before the clients on Price's books all need shoots for their next year's spring/summer collections and his life is consumed by work again. It's a change he's looking forward to—the promotion provided a much-needed boost—but he's in no rush to see the lazy pace of his life change.

They're shooting at an old fish camp that overlooks a glassy lake surrounded by picturesque pine trees. It reminds him of a place his parents rented one summer when he was a kid. They'd spent the week fishing and getting sunburned, and he'd had his first kiss: Becky Evans. She was two years older and wore braces accented with purple and teal rubber bands; she smelled of coconut from the sunscreen she needed whenever she ventured outside. It wasn't bad, as far as first kisses go, but it had not been Scott's ideal summer fling.

That same summer, Scott had seen a lifeguard named Troy naked and knew unequivocally that he'd rather have a summer romance with Troy than with Becky. He'd come out to his parents not long after that, and in retrospect, Scott realized that summer on the lake was the last time he truly felt like part of his own family. Not that the Parkers didn't love their youngest son; they just didn't fully understand. That year for Christmas, his dad bought him a flannel shirt from L.L. Bean and a hunting rifle. His mom got him a Cher CD.

The place where they're shooting reminds him of that odd mix of gifts. It's very L.L. Bean, but the contrast of the chic lines of Jan West's urban designs will be striking—as if someone had plucked Cher from the stage and plopped her in a rustic, rural scene. Something tells Scott that Jamie is going to love it.

Scott has thrown on a T-shirt and a simple pair of shorts. It's not something he'd wear to work on a normal day, but knowing he'll be outside and running around, well, it just seems as though he should make the exception for comfort's sake.

Jamie shows up a little before nine, just as Scott and Zach are setting up for the first shot. He walks up to Scott in long, purposeful strides, his black Wayfarers accentuating his sharp cheekbones and setting off the fairness of his complexion perfectly.

"Isn't this great?" Scott asks, feeling lighter and happier now that he sees Jamie. He wipes the sweat from his forehead with the back of his hand.

"Oh my God," Jamie says. "It's like a mosquito banquet out here, and I'm the main course." He swats at invisible bugs dramatically.

"We've got bug spray," Scott says, laughing. "And you'll be wearing long sleeves."

"Yes, that makes everything better. The mosquitoes won't get me but I'll sweat to death," he snarks. "Thank *heaven* for bug spray and long sleeves."

"And thoughtful crew members," Zach says, knowing full-well Scott brought the bug spray.

"He's just sucking up so I'll behave and we can get out of this heat as quickly as possible," Jamie replies, winking at Scott.

"So I guess you two made up," Zach says with a knowing look.

"Something like that," Scott replies, not looking up from his light meter.

Zach raises an eyebrow and asks, "Has anyone seen Yvonne?" obviously trying to change the subject.

"Oh," Scott says, fumbling with the light meter. "Um, she's not coming."

"She sick again?"

"I was… well, I was sort of promoted the other day. And um, well…"

"Oh my God, Scott, that's fantastic!" Jamie says, throwing his arms around him. Scott doesn't react for a second or two because he can't believe Jamie is hugging him. When he finally lifts a hand to press into Jamie's back, Jamie is already pulling away and refusing to make eye contact.

"Thanks," Scott says, running a hand along the back of his neck while Jamie bounces on the balls of his feet like an eager child.

"We should celebrate," Jamie says.

"Oh, you don't have to…"

"No, Scott," Jamie says. "This is a big deal. You have to celebrate, and it's my treat."

Scott presses his lips together and looks back and forth between Jamie and Zach.

"Come on," Jamie says. "Just one drink… with a friend. It's a major milestone in your career. You need to stop and appreciate it."

"But it's Friday night. I'm sure you already have plans."

"Well, I do," Jamie says, looking a little uncomfortable at the admission. "But that's not until later. I have time for *one* drink."

Scott isn't sure what he thinks of that piece of information. Jamie has plans, a date perhaps, but he wants to take Scott out first. As friends, he reminds himself before he can get too carried away.

"Zach?" Scott says. "Care to join us?"

"Can't, man," Zach replies, looking up from where he's kneeling. "The girlfriend will flip if I don't head straight home tonight. We haven't seen each other in three days." His mouth quirks up a bit as he returns his attention to his camera bag. "But uh, you kids have fun."

Jamie doesn't notice the look Zach is giving them and clasps his hands together excitedly. "So just you and me then. I have to go find Sheena and Isaac, but try and think of a place you'd want to go."

Jamie heads off toward the cabin. Scott's eyes follow him until he sees movement out of the corner of his eye. He looks down at

Zach who is shaking his head and laughing.

"From enemies to lovers just like that."

"We're just friends, Zach. It's not a date."

"Okay, okay," he says, standing up and dusting off his knees. "It's not a date. So then why are you blushing?"

"It's just hot out here," Scott replies. "Too much sun; not enough sunscreen."

"Oh, come off it. You're totally into him," Zach says. "And he's totally into you."

Scott looks up at him sharply. "He's really not."

"Please. The sexual tension between you two at the last shoot was so thick, you could cut it with a knife. Not to mention he's never been this friendly with anyone on set before besides David. He likes you, Scott." Zach brushes off his hands. "I need some water. You want?"

Scott nods, trying to look as nonchalant as possible while his mind floats into thoughts of Jamie and drinks after work. The snug-fitting jeans he'll wear that hug his ass just so, the way his hair will be styled perfectly to look like he didn't style it at all, his laughter bright and effortless as Scott charms him, the softness of his lips when he dares to steal a kiss.

Scott is pulled from his daydream by a muffled laugh.

"What's so funny?"

"You. All dreamy-eyed and ridiculous."

"I am not," Scott says petulantly.

"And still blushing," Zach adds. He brushes past Scott and leaves him staring open-mouthed.

* * *

Convincing Zach that he and Jamie are just friends might be easier than convincing his own racing heart, which picks up rapidly when he accidentally overhears a conversation between Jamie and Sheena.

"It's not like that. I asked him out strictly as friends. Co-workers even."

"Co-workers?" Sheena says. "Like *friendly* co-workers who occasionally hate each other and have to see one another in their underwear?"

Jamie scowls at her, and she laughs just as Scott steps around the corner and into the room.

"Technically speaking, Sheena, only one of us has seen the other in his underwear," Scott says, saving Jamie from the same embarrassing fate he himself had to endure with Zach.

Jamie's face flushes in the split second it takes him to realize that Scott overheard their conversation. "Stop rubbing it in, Scott," he says, quickly composing himself. "I was just telling Sheena about your promotion."

Jamie's teasing makes Scott smile.

"Congratulations," Sheena says. "Jamie says you're going out to celebrate."

"Yes, and I told her we're just friends. It's not a date," Jamie adds quickly.

"No, of course not," Scott says, his nerves returning now that Jamie seems flustered. "Jamie already has a date tonight, and it's certainly not me. Just a friendly celebratory drink."

He's rambling and he knows it, but it's like verbal diarrhea; it can't be stopped. He just needs to focus his thoughts on something. Anything. Manners. What is the polite thing to do? "In fact, you're free to join us," he blurts.

Sheena smiles at him, ignoring the way he'd practically shouted the invitation at her. "Thanks, but I've got to pick up the rugrat from her dad's and then it's our traditional Friday night Disney princess marathon. I lead an exciting life, I know. But you boys have fun."

Scott breathes a sigh of relief. Not that he doesn't like Sheena, but well, that's just too much pressure on him and Jamie for their first… time hanging out outside of work. God, why did he think first date? It's *not* a date.

He glances at Jamie, whose eyes are closed as Sheena finishes up his makeup. Wow, Jamie looks great in that blue sweater. Not a date, he reminds himself.

"See you later," he mumbles and leaves Jamie in Sheena's capable hands.

* * *

Scott suggests a hole-in-the-wall wine bar near his apartment, one of those places that serve wine in oversized glasses they only ever fill a third of the way, and charge twice the price just because they can. Scott picks it because it's familiar and he's a little nervous about being alone with Jamie again, though he tells Jamie that they have this really amazing wine and cheese pairing thing every Friday night. "You wouldn't believe how much better the wine tastes," he gushes.

Jamie looks unimpressed, but tells Scott he'll meet him there at seven. He has to go home and change for his date.

Scott gets to the bar first and grabs a small corner table, for absolutely no other reason than to avoid getting trampled on by people making their way to the bar.

The thing is, even though they both said it wasn't a date—because Jamie already has a date for the evening, and damn if that guy isn't the luckiest guy in town because Jamie looks amazing tonight—it *feels* like a date, thanks to Scott's sweaty palms and racing heart.

"I bought you something," Jamie says, slinking into his chair with a sly smile playing on his lips.

"You… what?"

"A gift," he says as if it's the simplest thing he'll ever do. "To celebrate your promotion."

He hands Scott a nondescript brown gift bag, overflowing with teal tissue paper, and a small card that reads, "To Scott… your friend, Jamie."

Scott looks up to smile at him and says, "Thank you."

Jamie rolls his eyes and playfully swats his knee. "You haven't even opened it yet, silly."

Scott's smile grows wider as he digs into the paper like a child on Christmas morning. His hands close around something soft—some sort of fabric. He tugs it out of the bag, the tissue paper falling to the floor at his feet, and finds a small, gray cotton bundle. Scott shakes it out to reveal a T-shirt sporting the phrase "crop it like it's hot" over a watermarked image of a crop tool.

When he glances at Jamie, he can see the giddy excitement in his eyes threatening to spill over. Scott can't help himself as he laughs loudly. "Oh my God, Jamie. This is perfect."

"I knew you'd like it," Jamie says, leaning back a little in his seat. He waves a waitress over. "I hope it fits. I kind of guessed at your size."

Scott holds it up to read the tag. "Looks like it'll be fine," he says. "Might be a little snug."

"I think you can pull it off," Jamie says with a shrug.

Scott is caught off guard by what could be construed as a compliment, but doesn't really have time to react or even say thank you, because the waitress has just asked Jamie what he wants to drink.

"I'll take your house Shiraz," he says.

The waitress looks at Scott. "Would you like another glass?"

Scott nods and hands her his empty wine glass. After an uncomfortable silence, Jamie breaks the tension.

"So tell me something I don't know about you," he says, leaning toward Scott with genuine interest in his eyes.

"Um, well..."

"Oh come on, Scott. Something juicy. Something you haven't told a living soul. Or wait. No... something embarrassing. A ridiculous college story about how you got drunk at a party and made out with a girl."

Scott puffs out a sharp laugh. "That never happened," he says, "but my first kiss was with this girl named Becky at summer camp."

"Really? Me too," Jamie says with a laugh. "Only it wasn't at summer camp, and her name was Amy. She was actually my best friend, and I was mostly trying to prove to this guy I had a crush on that I was straight."

"Did it work?" Scott asks growing more serious.

"Might have been more convincing if it hadn't happened *after* I came out."

"That might have been a giveaway, yeah," Scott says with a laugh.

There's a small, but electricity-charged moment where they make eye contact, both laughing at the same thing, and it feels like *something*. Like something magical is trying to take hold. A sudden rush of overwhelming emotion hits Scott hard—a thrilling jolt of new and exciting and perfect. He senses a fundamental shift, something undeniable about the way he sees Jamie, and he wishes he could take a moment to process what he's feeling, because he knows this moment is huge. But only if it's captured and cherished, is nourished and worshipped, will it grow to its full size. Only then will it expand and mature and become everything. And suddenly it hits him: Maybe it's more than a physical attraction that has him so obsessed with Jamie.

Scott forces himself to look away. He can't go there just yet, not with Jamie smiling at him, his eyes affectionate and warm.

He wills his thoughts back to the conversation, to what Jamie had just said about trying to be something you're not in order to protect yourself. A memory comes to him like a scene in a movie, only he's privy to the hateful sting of the emotion that went with it. Lonely, scared, feeling unwanted and judged by his parents, and then briefly "dating" his best friend Misty because it was easier than living the truth. He looks back at Jamie, hoping to find the moment isn't completely lost.

Jamie tilts his head to the side. "Something wrong?"

"I was just remembering a similar experience. I used my best friend as a beard when I was a junior in high school."

"How did that turn out?"

"She graduated; went to college, and I had to face the fact that I was gay when this guy Brad asked me out."

"Was he cute?"

"Sort of," Scott says. "He was prone to acne and wore braces, but he was sweet." Scott takes a sip of his wine and smiles at Jamie.

"And look how far you've come."

"Yeah, almost thirty and still single," he says. "Oh wow, I just realized I'm remembering something from high school that happened almost fifteen years ago, and you're thinking about something that probably happened last Tuesday. God, I'm old."

"You're not old," Jamie says. "And anyway, you *look* nineteen."

Scott raises his eyebrows at Jamie and purses his lips.

"Okay, twenty-four. But you're not old."

Jamie's phone buzzes and he picks it up off the table. "Shit."

"What is it?" Scott asks. "Something wrong?"

"I'm just having a really good time," he says.

"And you have to go," Scott says. He looks down, feeling genuine disappointment that they can't talk longer.

Jamie tilts his head and looks thoughtful for a moment before glancing down at his phone and typing out a response. He sets it down and grins at Scott. "I haven't even had my drink yet. He can wait a little while longer."

Scott feels something flutter in his chest. He tries to tamp it down because if he lets it unfurl and take flight, it might get away from him. So he convinces himself that maybe Jamie just doesn't want to be rude. Because anything more than that is just a little bit terrifying, and maybe, if he doesn't think about it too much, a little bit wonderful.

Still, a small part of him hopes Jamie is staying because he enjoys his company, that they really *can* be friends. Because this man, this striking god of a man, is too good to let go. How Scott knows that already is not something he's willing to address, even in his own inner ramblings.

As if on cue, their drinks arrive. Scott practically lunges for the fresh glass, needing the distraction of something to do with his hands. The waitress sets down the cheese plate he'd ordered before Jamie arrived and asks if they need anything else.

Scott's voice seems to be failing him, so he just shakes his head at the same time Jamie says, "No, thank you."

When they're alone again, Jamie's lips part around the rim of the wine glass as the deep burgundy liquid passes over them. His bottom lip is full and pouty where it grips the thin glass. Jamie's eyes close as he holds the wine in his mouth, savoring the flavor. Scott watches as his neck contracts and he swallows. It might be the most erotic thing he's ever seen.

"I'm so glad you wanted to do this, Scott," Jamie says as if he hadn't just been making love to his wine while Scott grew increasingly aroused sitting across from him.

Scott blinks a few times, trying to clear his head, and smiles at him. "Thank you for celebrating with me," he says, lifting his glass to Jamie.

"To new adventures," Jamie says.

"To new adventures," Scott replies, clinking his glass against Jamie's. They drink with their eyes locked, and Scott is certain it's another moment, but then Jamie's phone buzzes on the table and it's gone. Jamie glances at it and frowns.

"I'll be right back," he says. "I need to make a quick call."

Scott watches Jamie walk through the crowded bar and out the front door. From their tiny table he can just see him pacing the sidewalk in front of the bar's window while he talks. For a second, Scott sees Jamie's face, and he looks annoyed, but when Scott sees him again, he's walking back through the bar and smiling tentatively at Scott.

"So, I guess my date had to cancel," he says with a shrug.

"Oh, Jamie, I'm sorry."

Jamie waves him off. "It's okay," he says. "Just means you're stuck with me then."

"It would be my pleasure."

They order a bottle of wine and another cheese plate.

"So tell me about high school, Scott," Jamie says. "Were you out?"

"Not at first," he says, remembering what his first high school had been like. "I was kind of shy."

"You?" Jamie teases, mouth open in mock surprise. "Never."

"Shut up," Scott says. "Do you want to hear this story or not?"

Jamie gestures for him to continue while he takes another sip of wine. Jamie absently licks the rim of the glass and Scott has to avert his eyes to keep from tackling him there in the bar.

"So, as I was saying," he continues. "I didn't really come out at school until spring of my senior year. And uh… well, it was kind of tough for me before that anyway. I was teased, which led to bullying." He pauses and takes a deep breath. "Which led to getting my ass kicked by the fucking quarterback because he thought I was checking him out in the locker room."

"Oh my God," Jamie says. "That's awful."

"It was a long time ago," Scott reassures. "Anyway, after that my parents sent me to a private school, and I came out of my shell. That's where I met Misty. I joined the school's theater group, even had a boyfriend or two." He tips his glass in Jamie's direction and takes another sip.

"Here's to old zit-faced Brad," Jamie says, before drinking from his own glass.

"Shut up," Scott says. "He was sweet."

Jamie's eyes go wide and a playful grin lights up his face.

"You did theater?"

Scott nods.

"Are you any good?"

"Well, I was the lead in three musicals, back in the day," he says. "I can hold my own."

"Me too," Jamie says.

"You were the lead in three musicals?" Scott asks. Maybe the wine is dulling his senses a little.

Jamie laughs. "No, but I was in my high school's drama club. We did *The Wiz* my senior year."

"Small world," Scott says. "So did we. I was the Tin Man."

"I was the Scarecrow," Jamie says. "Although, I pulled a Rex Harrison and spoke most of my song because gospel wasn't my thing."

They sit talking for hours, discovering that they both grew up in the suburbs—Jamie outside St. Louis, Scott near Chicago. Jamie tells Scott that his father died when he was twelve; Scott tells Jamie how he always thought he lived in his older brother's shadow— until their server returns to ask if they want another bottle, which would actually be their third if Scott's counted correctly. His head is spinning and he's not quite sure he's ready to leave, but it's getting late.

"Um, maybe just our check," he says.

"It's on me," Jamie says, his words coming out slurred and giggly as he reaches for his wallet.

"Fine, but then you need to finish this cheese," Scott says as the waitress leaves, holding the plate out for Jamie to take.

"No way," he says, shaking his head to emphasize his point. "That will go straight to my hips, and I've had enough dairy to last me for the next month."

"Oh, come on," Scott says. "Your hips are fine. Trust me, I should know. I've spent hours staring at them."

"Of course they are," Jamie says. "Yoga, cardio six times a week..." Jamie trails off and gapes at Scott.

Realizing what he's accidentally revealed, Scott backpedals. "For work," he says. "I meant for work. I have to edit a lot of photos of you, and I have to retouch sometimes, and *your* hips? Well, they're just *not* problematic. That I've noticed." The truth is, he'd spent hours studying just how perfect Jamie's entire body is; none of it was anywhere near problematic.

"Oh right, work," Jamie says, waving off Scott's rambling. "Of course. I knew that."

Scott exhales and silence envelops them again, but this time, instead of a heated tension, it's like easing into a warm bath. Jamie's eyes are shining and bright. Scott just wants to lose himself in them.

"I should probably go," Jamie says suddenly. As he stands, he sways on his feet.

"Whoa," Scott says, reaching out for his hand and pulling him back into his chair. "Easy there."

"I'm fine," Jamie says. "Just caught up— I mean, *got* up too fast."

"I should probably call you a cab," Scott says.

"What about you?" Jamie says, pouting. He looks adorable and sexy, and if Scott doesn't get out of here soon, he's going to do something really stupid, like kiss him.

"I live within walking distance," Scott replies. "I'll be fine."

"Whereas I'm a hot mess," Jamie says, swaying in his seat.

"I wouldn't say that."

"Well, what would you say?" he asks.

Jamie smiles at him, eyelids heavy, lips flushed a deep pink from the wine. The heightened awareness he carries as a model is completely gone, and what's left is pure sex.

Scott swallows around the cotton-stuffed feeling in his mouth. If he says what he wants to say, it could be a turning point. That path is probably best left unexplored for now.

"I'd say we both need to sleep this off."

"Fine," Jamie says. "I just don't wanna go home."

"Well, I don't think you should have any more to drink tonight," Scott says.

"Easy, old man. That's not what I meant." Jamie hiccups and then laughs at himself. "I only meant I want to go to your place."

Scott is not sure what to think, but he knows Jamie is in no state to get himself home, and Scott's apartment is only three blocks away.

"Okay," he says, sounding far more shaky than he would like.

* * *

They stumble through the door. Scott drops his keys, and Jamie nearly falls on top of him as he bends to pick them up. Scott flips on the hall light and tries to extricate Jamie from his lightweight sweater, but they're both stumbling and Jamie is giggling and half asleep, and there are a lot of buttons. So Scott gives up and leads Jamie into the living room.

Jamie sits as Scott removes each of his boots gently. He eases Jamie down on the couch, careful to make sure a throw pillow is beneath his head. Then he grabs the fleece blanket from the back of the sofa and drapes it over Jamie's legs. The moment is intimate in the most innocent of ways, even as Scott realizes Jamie is lying in the very spot where he had fantasized about him only a week ago. Jamie's eyes flutter closed, and Scott is tempted to brush a stray hair from his forehead. He can't help but think that he'd rather have the real thing dozing off on his couch than a million sexual fantasies about a model he barely knows.

"Scott?" Jamie mutters, eyes closed and voice heavy with alcohol and sleep.

"Yeah."

"I'm really glad I canceled my date."

His breath catches. Did he hear that right? He waits, thinking Jamie might repeat himself or clarify. When Scott hears Jamie's breath even out, he's all but certain he's fallen asleep.

"Me too," he says into the darkness. "Goodnight, Jamie."

He resists the urge to kiss Jamie's forehead and stumbles to his bedroom, unsure if he's more drunk from the wine or from the realization that Jamie actually canceled his date to have drinks with him.

Chapter 6

When Scott wakes up, there's no sign of Jamie. Scott's heart sinks at the sight of the empty sofa and the absence of Jamie's shoes under the coffee table. It shouldn't feel so awful; Jamie probably had things to do and didn't want to bother him. But it still hurts because part of him had hoped he could make coffee and they could chat over blueberry pancakes.

But none of that is happening today, because Jamie is gone. The apartment is cold and dark; it feels empty despite Ben snoring in his bedroom. Scott runs his hands through his hair, wondering how long ago Jamie left. It's just a little after seven, still early. He might not be home yet.

He retreats to his bedroom to grab his phone.

Scott: *You make it home ok?*

Jamie: *Just walked through the door. Sorry about last night. I can be kind of clingy when I've been drinking.*

Scott doesn't remember clingy. He remembers stunning, witty, sexy, maybe a little giggly, but not clingy.

Scott: *No problem. You were a perfect gentleman and passed out about ten seconds after we walked in the door.*

Jamie: *Oh god. Sorry again.*

Scott: *It's fine. I'm just glad you got home safe.*

Jamie: *Perfectly safe, just hung over.*

Jamie: *Congrats again on the promotion.*

Scott: *Thanks! I had fun. We should do it again, but maybe stop after one bottle. ;)*

He's staring at his phone, willing a response to appear when Ben's voice echoes down the hallway.

"Saw you had an overnight guest," he says.

"He was drunk and I didn't want him going home alone."

"Easier to take advantage of that way," Ben says as he saunters into the living room, wearing only his boxers.

Scott feels his phone buzz in his hand, and glances down, hoping for a reply. It's only an email. "Shut up," he says, both to his phone and to his roommate.

"So is he as good in bed as you had hoped?"

"Nothing happened, Ben."

Scott thinks he sees a teasing smirk, but then Ben turns toward the kitchen and sets about making himself a cup of tea.

"You know, for someone who said he was going to start dating again," Ben says as he drops a tea bag in his mug, "you're really not doing too well. The least you can do is get a good fuck out of it."

"I'm not trying to date Jamie… or fuck him," Scott insists. "We're just friends."

Scott ignores the voice in the back of his mind telling him he screwed it all up; the voice grows even louder when he glances at his phone and still doesn't have a response to his last text.

"Well, if you keep hanging around with that Jamie guy, it's going to be hard for you to find a man. People will think you're together."

"Ben, I've told you a million times. Just because two gay men are speaking, it doesn't mean they're fucking."

"No, but the odds are in your favor."

Scott rolls his eyes. He can't handle Ben's teasing and a hangover too. He grabs his laptop off the coffee table and heads for the quiet of his bedroom.

* * *

Scott doesn't hear from Jamie for at least a week. He tries not to think about it too much because he doesn't think Jamie would appreciate him pushing the issue. Obviously he needs his space. Or maybe he hasn't given Scott or their night out another thought. What's odd is that Scott isn't really sure which scenario hurts less. The turning point turns out to be another random encounter, much like when he ran into Jamie at the club. Scott is standing in line for coffee, bleary-eyed and half awake, at a coffee shop he's never been to, on his way to a press check on the other side of town and in desperate need of caffeine.

"One medium, sickeningly black coffee." The voice washes over him like warm honey, bright and mildly sweet. It trickles down to his toes.

Scott turns to his right and sees Jamie looking more striking than he had dared to remember. His hair is high, swooped back from his face in its usual style, but it looks as if Jamie's gotten highlights since the last photo shoot. The bright flecks of gold bring out the rosy undertones of his complexion. Scott smiles.

"Hi, Scott."

"You bought me coffee," he says, incredulous.

"I saw you come in right before I ordered. Thought I'd save you some time."

"Thanks."

Scott steps out of line and takes the paper cup; the brush of Jamie's skin when their hands fleetingly touch comforts him a little.

"You got a second?" Jamie asks. The way he's looking at Scott—all wide eyes and expectant hesitation—makes him wish he hadn't hit snooze three times that morning.

"I'm kind of running late," he says.

Jamie's face falls, taking Scott's heart right along with it as if it were attached to Jamie's emotions by a thread.

"But I can spare a couple of minutes," Scott blurts out. "Someone saved me a little time by buying my coffee."

Jamie's closed-lip smile might be the cutest thing Scott has ever seen.

"I just wanted to apologize again about last week. I don't want you to think all I do is go out, get drunk and flirt with guys."

"I didn't think that."

"Right, well, I'd like to still be your friend," Jamie says. The fear of rejection in his eyes is so intense, Scott wants to wrap him in a tight hug. "If that's still an option."

Scott bites back a laugh as Jamie toys with his coffee cup.

"Jamie." He ducks down to meet Jamie's downcast gaze. "Our friendship is not dependent on how drunk or sober you are at any given time. Of course we're still friends."

Jamie shifts his gaze from his coffee cup, finding Scott's eyes and smiling tentatively. "I was just worried I made a fool of myself and you would think I was just some dumb kid who didn't know how to hold his booze."

Scott doesn't fight the laughter this time. "Are you kidding? I was just as drunk as you were."

"I wish I could remember," Jamie says. "I bet you were an even bigger dork."

"Not possible," Scott says.

"That's true. You're a pretty big dork sober."

"You really don't remember *anything* from the other night?"

"No," Jamie says. "Why? Did something happen?"

"Nothing to be embarrassed about," Scott reassures. "You're kind of adorable when you're drunk." And you canceled your date to be with me, Scott adds mentally. He's thought about that so much he's surprised he didn't just blurt it out and embarrass them both.

Jamie's expression wavers, his eyes unable to focus on any one part of Scott's face, as if he's caught somewhere between flattered and embarrassed.

The irresistible pull Scott always feels when they lock eyes comes back in full force when Jamie finally looks at him, spurring him to say something. Should he ask Jamie if he feels it too, and seek reassurance that he's not alone in this overwhelming sense of being right where he should be? He needs to know if Jamie senses the magnetic force of the world spinning around them, stopping and holding them in place. Does Jamie feel the same rush of ecstasy from these moments?

"Listen, I've, uh, got to run, but did you want to maybe get coffee again tomorrow? I can meet you here at, say…" He checks his watch. "Eight-thirty?"

"I'd like that," Jamie says, looking at Scott fondly. Scott feels warm all over, the string on his heart tugging skyward, as though it might float away.

"Okay. See you then."

When his hand hits the door, he turns back, admiring the way Jamie adjusts the leather bag on his shoulder, making sure his shirt isn't wrinkled. When he twists to check the back of his red pants, Scott notices how the sheen of the waxed denim highlights every inch of his legs. He's perfect, of course, but what Scott finds most endearing is all the vulnerability that Jamie works so hard to conceal.

"Oh, and Jamie."

"Yeah?"

"You're not some dumb kid."

* * *

It's surprising how natural—inevitable, almost—it seems when Jamie starts calling or texting Scott at random moments. And Scott can't help but send Jamie photos of projects he's working on: sneak peeks at spring lines of designers who have booked Price to work on their campaigns, location possibilities for upcoming shoots, hideous logo ideas. Jamie responds to them all, offering opinions that are often scathing and, on rare occasions, gushing with praise.

A last-minute movie night at Scott's apartment—because Jamie had never seen *Vertigo*, and Scott couldn't imagine not having seen every Hitchcock movie ever made—becomes the first in a series of not-dates, with Jamie and Scott relying on each other for company because their schedules are too unpredictable for anything else. They also meet for coffee pretty much every morning, even though it's about fifteen minutes out of Scott's way.

"I'm sorry about dinner last night," Jamie says over their usual Tuesday lunch, when Tuesday lunches have somehow become something they do together, as well as regular movie nights at Scott's apartment and the occasional outing with mutual friends. For some reason, everyone thinks they're dating. Scott doesn't understand it. He's been careful to tell anyone who asks him that he and Jamie are just friends. "I didn't think that shoot would run quite so long."

"It's okay. I fell asleep on the couch around ten anyway."

"No wonder we're both single." Jamie exaggerates an eye roll, making Scott laugh. *He's* definitely single, but it's not as if Jamie doesn't have prospects. Now that Scott thinks about it, Jamie spends most of his free time with him. It seems odd that he'd want to spend so much time with a friend when he could be dating.

"What about that guy who canceled? He ever reschedule? If I'm cramping your style—"

Jamie shifts nervously in his seat and says, "Oh, I don't think that's really going anywhere."

"Too bad."

"What about you?" Jamie asks. "Any hot dates on the horizon?"

Huffing out a laugh, Scott just shakes his head. "Chronically single. I haven't been on a date that was remotely promising in… oh, two years."

"I find that hard to believe."

"It's true. My ex always said I have impossibly high standards."

"Do you?"

Scott thinks about it, wondering if Jacob had been right. "I'm not sure," he says finally. "I like to think I'm just waiting for Mister Right."

Jamie suddenly looks sullen, and Scott has a fleeting urge to make him smile again. "You're one to talk," he says. "Mister 'I don't date industry people.' What's that all about anyway? I'm guessing your date from the other night wasn't another model."

Jamie hums noncommittally, and Scott decides not to push for more. If Jamie remembers next to nothing of the night he stayed over, Scott can't even be sure that what Jamie had said about canceling the date was true. Jamie had been drunk, after all. They've never talked about it, and he doesn't want to embarrass Jamie by bringing it up. Or worse, giving Jamie the impression that Scott thinks he's a liar. Besides, maybe he's reading too much into it. It's entirely possible that Jamie wasn't really interested in the guy to begin with and had been looking for an excuse to cancel. Celebrating a friend's promotion was an easy out; Scott's probably fixating on it for nothing.

Reminded of work by his thought, Scott glances at his watch. "Shit, I'm going to be late." He picks up his dirty tray and grabs his computer bag. "Oh, by the way, Yvonne says they're doing a special screening of *Gone with the Wind* at the Trocadero on Friday. Do you want to go?"

"Do you even have to ask?" Jamie asks. "Clark Gable, gorgeous costumes, high drama. If that doesn't scream Jamie Donovan, I don't know what does."

"How silly of me," Scott teases. "I should have known."

"Meet you there at seven?" Jamie asks, picking up his bag from the back of his chair.

"Sure. Dinner after?" Scott suggests as he throws away his trash. "Of course."

Scott holds the door for Jamie, watching him until he turns the corner, before heading in the opposite direction, humming.

* * *

Scott finds himself humming a lot—in the shower, on the subway, at work. In fact, he's doing it when a scowling Sheena bombards him the second he gets to the photo shoot the following Monday.

"Good morning, Scott," Sheena says. "Isaac says we have a couple new guys starting today."

"Oh yeah, sorry. I thought you knew," he says. "Adamo and, uh… Preston, I think."

She sighs heavily and pushes her blue-tinged hair off her forehead. "Don't worry. We'll make it work," she says.

"I know you will," Scott says, kissing her on the cheek. "That's why you're my favorite."

"Stop trying to butter me up and just promise me you'll send them into hair and makeup as soon as they get here. We're going to be pressed for time as it is."

"Of course. Anything you want," he says. "You're a doll."

Sheena smiles and waves him off, leaving Scott to begin setting up.

Jan West had insisted on group shots to fill out the holiday campaign. So Scott and Yvonne hired two new models. Adamo, a striking Italian, with gorgeous olive skin and glossy, dark hair, who speaks next to no English, communicates almost exclusively in clichéd pick-up lines and movie quotes. The other model, Preston, is a lanky brunet who spent the better part of the last two years working in Europe and makes a point of telling everyone. Yvonne had rolled her eyes at Scott when he had been hesitant to hire Preston because the model kept winking at him during the casting.

"Suck it up," she'd said. "He's hot."

Scott still isn't quite sure what to make of Preston when he introduces himself at the photo shoot.

"Oh, you're much sexier than my last art director," Preston says, grinning lasciviously at Scott. "Preston Worth. Very nice to meet you." He holds out a hand.

"Scott Parker. We met at the casting."

"I know," Preston says, winking.

"Right," Scott says. "Um, you need to get to hair and makeup right away." He points over Preston's shoulder. "We're kind of running behind already." "See you later, gorgeous," Preston says and walks away, leaving Scott feeling as if Preston might as well have smacked him on the ass.

"Oh, my God. What are *you* doing here?"

Scott turns at the sound of Jamie's voice and sees him talking to Preston, a look of abject horror on Jamie's face.

"Hey, princess," Preston says. "What a small world. You just book this job too?"

"I've been working with this client for *weeks*," Jamie replies, shoulders back and head high.

"Guess they wanted a *new* look," Preston says.

"Yeah, I hear the douchebag look is all the rage this spring," Jamie replies. He crosses his arms and looks down his nose at Preston the way he had at Scott when they'd first met.

Scott bristles for reasons he can't quite understand. Why should it bother him if Jamie's just as rude to Preston as he was to Scott? It's just how he is with everyone new on set. No, not everyone, Scott thinks, just me.

Scott doesn't want to think about why that bothers him.

"Gentlemen," he says, composing himself. "We need to get you both into hair and makeup ASAP. You can bicker in there."

Jamie glares at Scott but heads off immediately; Preston stays behind. He looms over Scott, which is intimidating, and the look on his face makes Scott think Preston is fully aware of how unnerving it is.

"You're sexy when you take charge," he says, smirking.

"Uh, thank you," Scott says. He's not really sure what else to say, but he's flattered by Preston's attention. Even if it does make him uncomfortable in a way he didn't expect. And then Preston is gone. Scott's heart is racing and he's not really sure why.

Scott doesn't have much time to dwell on Preston, though, because he's running behind most of the day, and well, Jamie is acting strange.

"Scott, would you mind getting me a towel?" he asks, while Zach moves some lights.

"Uh, sure."

It's the first time Jamie's accepted Scott's assistance on set, let alone asked for it. Scott tries not to consider the reasons behind it, handing over the towel and watching Jamie as he makes a show of running his hand along Scott's wrist, eyes on Preston the whole time.

Jamie gives him a soft "thanks" and a too-bright smile. The playful light in Jamie's eyes makes Scott's heart flutter with anticipation. Like maybe Jamie should always look at him this way. There's too little time to indulge in such thoughts, though. Between Adamo's inability to follow simple directions and Preston's blatant flirting, Scott spends most of the day feeling as if he's playing catch up. They don't even get through all of the shots Scott had planned.

Jamie's behavior is what really has Scott's head spinning, though. He goes out of his way to touch him whenever he can, always making sure Preston is watching. Meanwhile, Preston is doing his best to catch Scott's attention. Jamie seems to double his efforts whenever Preston is being particularly smarmy. It would be comical, if Scott weren't so stressed already.

"Scott, can you help me with this zipper?" Preston asks, struggling with his fly. "I don't know what's wrong with it."

"Isaac!" Jamie shouts. "Worth needs help with his pants!" He turns to Scott. "Could you get me some water?"

Isaac calls Preston over and Scott hands Jamie his water. There are no lingering touches or flirty giggles this time, though. Just an urgent tug on his sleeve.

"Scott, listen," Jamie says quietly. "I need to tell you something."

"What's up?" Scott asks.

"It's about Preston," he whispers, glancing over to where Isaac is examining Preston's fly.

"Okay."

Jamie leans in and says, "Don't go out with him, please."

"Not that he's asked, but why not?"

"Just… don't," Jamie says, picking at the label on the water bottle and not making eye contact. "Preston is…" Jamie looks up mid-sentence, and his eyes go wide. He clamps his mouth shut before shooting a panicked look to Scott.

"What about me, sweetheart?" Preston says, throwing an arm around Jamie. "You boys aren't fighting over me, are you?" He gives Jamie a playful smack on the ass, then leans toward Scott and winks. "Plenty of me to go around if you're into that sort of thing."

Scott glances at Jamie, who looks as though he can't decide if he wants to disappear or throw up. Does Jamie have a crush on Preston? Maybe he's worried Scott might swoop in and steal him.

"Jesus Christ, Preston, you're always in my face," Jamie sneers, shoving him away.

Or maybe not.

"We'll talk later," Jamie says into Scott's ear as he brushes past.

Preston's eyes follow Jamie until he's out of earshot. "So, you and the ice queen?" he asks, moving even closer to Scott.

"Sorry… what?" Scott furrows his brow as he turns back to Preston, unsure what to make of Jamie's behavior.

"You and Jamie look pretty… close," Preston says.

"Oh, well, we're friends," Scott offers.

"*Just* friends?"

Scott's beginning to wonder why no one believes him. Nothing has happened between him and Jamie, and Preston barely knows him. "Yes," he replies, tilting his head to the side. How could Preston possibly have an idea about his feelings?

"Good, because I'd like to get your number," Preston says. "Maybe we could go out some time."

"Oh Preston, that's very sweet, but I don't think–"

Preston interrupts, holding a hand up and letting it graze Scott's chest playfully. "You don't have to answer that now. Let's just exchange numbers and see where that leads, okay?"

Scott considers the suggestion. He's pretty sure he's not interested in dating Preston, but the man is undeniably handsome. Tall and muscular like a swimmer, with piercing gray eyes. It couldn't hurt to get to know him a little better, and it is flattering to be hit on so forcefully by someone younger.

"Yeah, sure. I suppose that would be okay," he says, handing Preston his phone. "But, um, I'm not really looking to date any-one." It's a lie, but Scott is just so used to protecting himself it's almost reflex.

"Who said anything about dating?" Preston replies while he enters his number and sends himself a text. "There, now I have yours too."

He hands Scott his phone and grins wolfishly. "I'll be in touch."

Scott stares after him, immediately regretting his decision to hand Preston his phone. Something about the way Preston is pursuing him feels wrong. It isn't as though Scott hasn't been propositioned before, blatantly. In college, Scott got hit on at least once a week, and, hell, his entire relationship with Jacob had started out as a one-night stand. But Preston, well, he seems more aggressive than what Scott is used to. Or maybe it's the way Jamie reacted. Eventually, he decides it's just a phone number and maybe nothing will come of it. Preston will probably pick up some guy at a bar and forget all about the short, dorky, tattooed art director with unruly hair and feet that are too big for his body.

When Scott glances up to see Jamie glaring at him, he *really* wishes he hadn't felt the need to be so polite.

* * *

Jamie avoids Scott for the rest of the day, shooting daggers at him and Preston whenever they speak to each other. Scott really doesn't like the gnawing feeling that's taken up residence in his chest. Everything feels wrong and he just wants to talk to Jamie, find out what's bothering him.

"Jamie, didn't you want to talk to me?" Scott asks when everything is packed up and Jamie looks as though he's rushing to get home. "About Preston?" he adds.

"Never mind," Jamie says, shoving things into his bag and not making eye contact. He's seething. Scott can see it, but he doesn't know what to do or say. "It's nothing. Just forget it."

"Jamie, what's wrong?"

"I just…" Jamie begins. Then he shakes his head as if he can't believe Scott is so oblivious. "I can't believe you gave your number to Preston Worth." He looks down at his hands and picks absently at his cuticles. It's the first time Scott's seen Jamie look his age. It's surprisingly beautiful.

He can't figure out why Jamie is back to being cold with him. Scott thought he and Jamie were friends, good friends, in fact. This shift feels like he's back to square one. Then again, what if Jamie does have a crush on Preston? Scott feels instantly guilty that he might have hurt Jamie's feelings in some way because of his stupid inability to say "no thank you."

"I'm sorry, Jamie. I didn't know you liked him."

"Oh my *God*," Jamie says, huffing out a breath on the last syllable. He turns on his heel just as Scott grabs him by the wrist.

"Don't be embarrassed, Jamie," he says softly, releasing Jamie's wrist and placing his hand gently on his arm. "We've all had crushes before. If you like him, I'll back off."

"Don't do me any favors," Jamie says, yanking his arm away.

"I'll see you tomorrow."

Scott notices that Jamie's shoulders sag as he walks away, his usually perfect posture faltering. He's shocked at how badly he wants to run after Jamie and try to make it all better.

* * *

The problem with booking Adamo and Preston is they're easily three to four inches taller than Jamie, and the height difference is pronounced whenever they're in group shots. Scott will have to do a lot of extra work to correct the difference.

Scott opens a few images on his computer and starts narrowing them down for Lorelei's approval.

It's different editing photos of Jamie now that they're friends. He can see little hints of Jamie's natural expressions in his "model" faces; his near-perfect posture is still there, but he's more relaxed when he's laughing at a joke or taking a sip of his chai. His slightly messier hair, a hint of stubble, a pair of lived-in jeans—all of it matches what Scott now knows about the real Jamie, and it thrills him. It's almost as if Jamie Donovan is two separate people, and Scott can't quite decide which one he finds more intriguing.

Both are stunning.

"Whoa," Yvonne says over his shoulder. "You were swimming in hot guys yesterday."

"Classy, Yvonne… as always."

"I'm just saying, you've got some serious eye candy there." Yvonne sits down at her desk and leans back. Scott doesn't look up. "What's got you so uptight?" she asks. "Did our Ivy League prepster hit on you again?"

Scott chuckles. Yvonne is frighteningly perceptive. "Gave me his number," he says, turning to face her. "Kind of forced it on me, actually. It was an… *interesting* experience to say the least."

Yvonne lifts an eyebrow. "So are you going to go out with him?"

"I don't know," Scott says. "Probably not."

"Why not?"

Scott shrugs. "I'm not really interested."

"*Scott*, he's hot," she says.

He shrugs again. "So?"

"He's hot, and he's available and he likes you. How could you not be interested?"

"He's just not my type, Yvonne," Scott says, focusing again on his screen. "And anyway, Jamie seemed kind of bothered by it."

"Jamie?"

"Yeah. I think maybe he's interested in Preston."

"Right… Preston," she mumbles into her coffee mug. "Maybe he's just jealous."

"That's what I'm saying," Scott says, turning back to face her.

"No, not because of Preston," Yvonne says, looking at him over the rim of her glasses. "Because of *you*."

"Me?"

"Mm hmm," Yvonne says, taking a drink of her coffee. "Did it ever occur to you that Jamie doesn't want Preston hitting on you because *he* likes you?"

"Oh that's ridiculous. We're just friends."

Yvonne rolls her eyes.

"We are," Scott insists. "He's a *kid*, Yvonne. He's nineteen, and I'm practically middle-aged."

"Watch it," she says. "I'm pushing forty."

"You know what I mean."

"Yeah, I do," she says, her face softening. "But age is just a number, Cupcake. And you're a good-looking single guy with a great job. There's no way that escaped his attention."

"You make it sound like he's shopping for a car."

"Stop deflecting. Is it really such a stretch?" she asks. "I mean, you like him, right?"

"That's completely beside the point."

Scott turns his chair back toward his desk and clicks around on his screen, trying to force himself to get back to work.

"No, Scott," Yvonne says. "That's kind of exactly the point."

Scott freezes.

"Why are you fighting this?" Yvonne asks quietly.

"I don't know," he replies, tamping down the growing feeling that Jamie has upended his entire world. He's not ready to face that yet—not at work anyway.

"Well, you need to figure that out, Scott," she says. "For both our sakes."

Chapter 7

"Jamie, please call me back. I want to explain."

It's the third message Scott's left on Jamie's voice mail, plus five text messages, all variations on the same theme: *I'm sorry. Please call me back. I haven't called Preston.*

But Jamie doesn't call. There are no text messages. Jamie had skipped their Tuesday lunch after the disastrous photo shoot, and Scott hadn't seen him in days. He'd found out from David that Jamie had gotten a cold and later learned from Sheena that it had developed into pneumonia, so Scott doesn't see him at work for weeks either.

Preston, on the other hand, is omnipresent. And he wants Scott to know it.

"So, hot stuff, you want to grab a drink after we finish up tonight?" Preston asks Scott with his usual smirk.

It's the second shoot Jamie's missed, and Scott is already feeling uneasy, almost as though his skin is the wrong size for his body. And his promise to Jamie remains at the forefront of his thoughts, keeping him from accepting the invitation despite his habitual courtesy.

But Preston is undeterred; his advances persist day after day, regardless of Scott's endless refrain of "no thank you."

The longer Jamie's gone—and not returning Scott's calls—the more the feeling of unease gives way to plain old loneliness, and after a tongue lashing from Ben about how he's still not "putting himself out there," Scott considers one of Preston's offers of lunch. Then he sees Preston flirting with Zach's assistant only moments later, and is even more determined to steer clear of him. Preston is obviously not interested in friendship or dating, and there's still the issue of Jamie.

"Preston, I appreciate the offer for lunch," he says, "but I've got some work to catch up on, and I think I'll call Jamie to see how he's feeling."

If the disdain Preston shows at the mention of Jamie's name is any indication, Scott made the right choice. He can't betray Jamie by befriending Preston, let alone dating him.

"You don't really know Jamie that well, do you?" Preston asks, his lips twisting into a gross parody of a smile.

"I'm sorry?" Scott says.

Preston sighs. "Me too," he says. "He'll never give it up, you know. He doesn't do casual sex."

Scott doesn't bother to tell Preston he's not looking for casual sex either because it's none of his business. Casual sex is easy to come by. He'd much rather have an actual relationship—the closeness, the intimacy, the comfort. His mind wanders back to Jamie. In just a few weeks, Jamie had become one of Scott's closest friends. He can tell Jamie things his straight friends would never understand. He'd forgotten what it was like to have another gay man to talk to; most of the guys he used to hang out with were really Jacob's friends, and when they broke up, the friends disappeared too.

After Preston walks away, Scott suddenly realizes he misses Jamie terribly; knowing that Jamie might still be upset with him makes it all somehow worse.

Scott picks up his phone, which has become an overwhelming backlog of unanswered texts and voicemails, and debates calling Jamie again. For the last few weeks, he's been neglecting what friends he does have by only responding to work-related emails, and, in general, declining every offer to grab dinner, drinks, or coffee with anyone who's not Jamie.

He knows he really should make an effort to see his other friends, but he doesn't want to.

Scott notes three texts from Preston, each one an invitation to dinner. Preston is clearly interested. Regardless of how Jamie feels about him, Preston doesn't seem to feel the same way. But it's Jamie. So Scott deletes Preston's texts. He sets his phone down, promising himself he'll respond to his brother about going out with him and a few friends for his birthday. He never does.

Meanwhile, Preston's comment about Jamie niggles at the back of his mind the entire week, eating away at his resolve until it comes to a head the day after Scott's thirtieth birthday. Without Jamie's presence to distract him, or even a text to wish him a happy birthday, Scott had fallen deep into a pit of self-loathing and loneliness, drinking a bottle of wine by himself and passing out on his sofa at midnight while waiting for Ben to get home.

Thanks to that night, the next time Preston asks him out, his guard is down.

"Scott, when are you going to give in and go out on one little, harmless date with me?"

The thought of spending another Friday night alone seems downright pathetic, and when Scott glances up and makes eye contact with Preston for the first time that day, he looks hopeful, all traces of the usual predator gone. That's new. "Are you free tonight?" Scott asks.

Preston's face lights up.

* * *

"So what changed your mind, Scott?" Preston asks, glancing over his glass at Scott with gleaming eyes.

Scott takes a deep breath. "To be honest, I'm not quite sure."

It's a lie, of course. He's here to prove something to himself—and to Ben—about his feelings for Jamie, about his own sanity. He's lonely and bored; he's also worried he's become too attached to his new friend. A man—no not a man, a *boy*—who is too young for him. He needs to remember that. He looks up at Preston who, at twenty-seven, is much closer to his own age.

"Wow, way to flatter a guy."

He's being sarcastic, of course. Not that it matters. Preston has a body that Scott wouldn't mind exploring with his hands and tongue. The only problem is, Preston acts as if he knows it. It's a bit of a turn-off and leaves Scott with an uncomfortable, queasy feeling in his gut.

"No, that's not what I meant," Scott says. "I mean, well, you're an attractive guy, Preston, and I'm not getting any younger. I'd be crazy not to give you a shot."

Scott takes another swig from his Jack and Coke, the heat of the liquor making his face feel warm and flushed.

"So I'm like a pre-midlife crisis date?"

"No, no," Scott insists, dropping his head in mild embarrassment at insulting Preston twice in the last minute. "It's hard to explain, but … Okay, have you ever had a moment in your life where you thought 'What am I waiting for?' Like you realized you needed to seize the moment or something?"

"Maybe," Preston says. "So this is you seizing the moment?" He looks confused and yet somehow bored, as if he doesn't quite care about the answer.

Scott considers his inquiry anyway. Is this a moment worthy of seizing? Is Preston worth it? Jamie is so young and he and Scott are just friends. Even in his mind, he can almost taste the bitterness of the word "friend," but acknowledging his feelings for Jamie is out of the question. He's fantasized and ogled for far too long, and it's all a bit too much for his brain to handle at the moment, so he shoves it aside.

With Preston there and Jamie pushed to the back of his mind, it's easy to rationalize his decision.

"Well, yeah."

Another lie. What he's really thinking about is seizing one of those moments with Jamie. Taking a chance when the sparks fly and the heat between them sizzles and pops. Convincing himself that he's talking about taking a chance with Preston becomes easier without the quiet thrill of Jamie's imagined presence to remind him.

"I can work with that," Preston says.

Scott looks down at his drink and rolls the glass in his hand, watching the deep amber liquid swirl around the ice cubes. He might as well make the most of the evening. "So how did you get into modeling?" he asks, taking a bite of his salad. "Was it planned or did you just stumble on it like Jamie?"

Preston's calm expression falters at another mention of Jamie's name, but only for a fraction of a second. "A little of both," he says.

"So you had a *plan* to stumble on it?" Scott teases.

"Something like that. My agent is actually a friend of the family. He'd been bugging me for years. So I lucked out a little bit in the beginning, but I do actually want to be a model."

"Are you into fashion?" Scott asks, thinking yet again about Jamie.

"No, I'm in it for the hot guys," Preston says, pointing his fork at Scott. "Being a model makes it easier to get laid."

Preston winks, and Scott coughs as a piece of mushroom catches in his throat.

"I-is that an important thing to you?" Scott sputters before wiping his mouth with his napkin.

Preston chuckles. "Sex?" Scott nods, and Preston continues, "Well, I am a fan." His smile is teasing, playful.

Scott chews slowly, unsure of what to say. He can't argue the point. Sex, as a rule, is something Scott enjoys. The idea of no-strings-attached sex had never been his particular cup of tea, but he'd never begrudge someone else the indulgence. Scott has always been of the mindset that as long as it's consensual, people should do what they want in bed—or anywhere else for that matter. And really, Preston could have just about any guy he wants. It makes sense. Even so, Preston's cavalier attitude seems so foreign to him, that Scott can't help but wonder if his own opinion of Jamie is entirely accurate.

"What did you mean when you said I don't really know Jamie?"

Preston sets his fork down with a sigh and steeples his hands under his chin. "Has he ever told you anything about himself?"

"Some things, yes," Scott says quickly, feeling defensive. Jamie has obviously kept things from him, but Preston doesn't need to know that.

"But nothing of real substance, right?"

Preston takes Scott's silence as confirmation.

"I'm just saying, he doesn't let people get close. You don't know him. Trust me, I've seen it before."

Scott looks down at his plate, moving an olive around with his fork. He doesn't want to dwell on how much more Preston might know about Jamie. He's also afraid if he continues to think or talk about Jamie, his feelings will be on full display for Preston to mock, or worse, tell Jamie.

"So tell me something about you," Scott says, changing the subject again. It feels like a betrayal to consider getting information on Jamie from someone else, even if it would help to fill in some of the holes in Jamie's story. He can wait for Jamie to tell him.

Grinning as though he's won some prize, Preston answers, "My father's an attorney. He married my mother for her money, which she used to buy new tits after she used it to bag a husband. I have an older sister, Jacqueline. She's at Harvard Law, living out the family dream and hating every minute of it. I'm the gay disappointment of a son who's only accepted in the social scene because he made it big as a model and Mommy Dearest can show me off to all her over-medicated Junior League harpies. I let them gush about my washboard abs while they talk about how their husbands are all on Viagra so they can fuck their secretaries stupid. Meanwhile, *I'm* usually fucking their closeted sons or hetero-flexible pool boys."

Scott bites his lip, but a laugh escapes.

"It's okay," Preston says. "You can laugh. It's ridiculous even to me, and I live it."

"Reminds me a little of my family," Scott confesses with a genuine smile. Suddenly Preston doesn't seem so bad.

"Ooh, intrigue."

"It's really not that exciting," Scott insists. "Nothing as dramatic as your story, but I come from a family with some money and a certain level of social prestige. My father's response to me coming out was, 'Not my son.' My mother asked if I was sure."

"Sounds about right," Preston says with a knowing nod. "Any siblings?"

"Just an older brother, Chris. He's much more accepting of the gay thing. In fact, he asks about my sex life with embarrassing frequency—like he's trying to prove that he's okay with it."

"At least he tries," Preston says, looking sad. "My sister just kind of ignores my sexuality altogether. As if it doesn't exist."

"That sucks," Scott says.

"Well, she's a bitch, so no loss there," Preston replies with a laugh, but his expression is at odds with his jovial tone. Maybe there's more to Preston than venom. It reminds him of Jamie.

The rest of the meal is actually nice. Preston is funny and charming and he even pays the check.

"I had fun," Scott says as they exit the restaurant.

"Well, no one said the night has to end, Scotty. How about we check out this club nearby? I know the DJ and I could probably score us some free drinks."

Scott checks his watch.

"It's Friday," Preston says, covering Scott's watch with his palm.

"Yeah, okay," he says. "Why not?" Besides, Scott can relate to Preston in a way, and he can tell neither of them wants to go home alone yet. Too much like their childhoods—home alone while everyone else is out living their lives.

The club is more brightly lit than Scott is used to, but the music is good and Preston is a pretty good dancer. There are shots and laughter, dancing and more shots, and flirting, which leads to kissing.

Preston leans in first, tentatively, as if he's asking for Scott's permission, but then becomes more confident when he doesn't meet any resistance. Scott tries not to think about it too much; Preston's tongue feels nice, and his muscles are firm under Scott's hands where they grip at his sides. The kisses grow more heated until Scott pulls back panting and looks up to find Preston's face flushed and his pupils wide with arousal.

"Let's go to my place," Preston says into his ear. His voice is low, a hot breath tickling Scott's neck.

"But we're dancing," Scott says, straining to be heard over the thrumming bass line.

"It's getting crowded," Preston says, fanning himself. "And hot. Come on ... let's get out of here."

Scott feels the sheen of sweat on his face and back acutely. Why hadn't he noticed that before?

"Um, okay," he says.

Preston grins at him and grabs him by the hand, leading him off the dance floor and toward the door.

Scott barely notices how they get to Preston's apartment, focusing instead on the pavement beneath his feet. His head is swimming and the air feels cool on his face.

"This is me," Preston says, holding a door open for Scott to walk through. They climb three flights of stairs and Preston pulls out his keys. No sooner are they're through the door than Preston's mouth is on Scott's, his tongue forcing its way between his parted lips when Scott gasps.

Scott kisses back out of instinct, letting the feeling wash over him, until finally his alcohol-soaked brain catches up.

"I think I need a drink of water," he rasps.

"Mmm," Preston murmurs. "Your mouth doesn't feel dry." His lips are on Scott's again and then trailing down his neck.

Scott moans when Preston finds a sensitive spot behind his ear.

"You like that?" Preston nips at it with his teeth, and Scott moans louder.

"God, I bet you're a talker," Preston says between kisses. He grips Scott's shirt in his hands and tugs it free of his pants, trailing his palms up and down Scott's back.

When Preston's hand presses into the small of Scott's back and then drifts down to cup his ass, he freezes.

"Preston, stop," he says, tapping him on the shoulder.

"Huh?" Preston mumbles, his tongue tracing a pattern on Scott's ear.

"Stop." His voice is louder this time, more firm.

Without backing away from him, Preston stops licking his ear, and his hands still. "Seriously?"

When Preston doesn't get a response right away, he presses a small kiss to Scott's neck. "Come on... doesn't this feel good?"

He squeezes Scott's ass again.

"Not tonight," Scott says.

Preston's left hand reaches down and cups Scott's crotch, smiling when he finds Scott half hard. "You don't mean that," he says.

"It's just a little too fast," Scott says, pushing on Preston's shoulders.

Preston doesn't move, though. His eyes are flashing with something that makes Scott's pulse race. The alcohol is buzzing sharply in his veins, making his mind swim and his body tingle with sensation.

"I can slow down if you like," Preston says, dragging his fingertip along Scott's cheek and pressing a soft kiss to his neck. "I can be whatever you need me to be. Just let me touch you."

Preston removes his hands from Scott's lower half, but stays well within his personal space, bringing his hands up to frame Scott's body against his front door. He towers over Scott and is looking down at him, his grey-green eyes burning with a passion Scott hasn't seen in him before. When Preston leans in to kiss him, Scott kisses back despite his better judgment. It's been so long since anyone wanted him this badly.

Before he can think, Preston's hand is on his fly, unzipping his jeans and slipping his hand down the front of his tiny boxer-briefs. It feels so good to be touched like that, he can't even think about trying to hold back the moan that escapes his lips.

"Yeah, I knew you'd like it," Preston rasps.

Aroused and barely in control of his own body, Scott grips Preston's shoulders for leverage as he lets his tongue explore Preston's neck. It earns him a hum of pleasure and a tighter grip on his dick.

Falling to his knees, Preston pulls Scott's jeans down around his ankles and grins lasciviously at his bright purple underwear. "Of course you're a Calvin Klein man."

"You were expecting something else?"

"I wasn't expecting anything. It's just predictable."

Before Scott can protest the slight, Preston has pulled down his Calvins just enough to press his hot, persistent mouth to the head of Scott's cock. Hissing out a sharp breath, Scott arches his back, his head thudding against the door.

He loses himself in pleasure, his only thought of release. Closing his eyes, Scott can almost imagine himself somewhere else—with *someone* else.

Preston moans and it brings him crashing back into reality, but it's too late. His orgasm is building and Preston is speeding up, his mouth and hand driving Scott rapidly over the edge. As he comes, Scott bites back a name that would betray him too much. His head falls against the door again, the only sounds his heaving breaths and Preston's self-satisfied chuckle.

"Always a showstopper," he jokes, wiping the back of his hand lewdly across his mouth.

Without the haze of arousal to cloud his judgment, Scott feels the sting of regret wash over him like a frigid bucket of water. "Oh shit … what was I thinking?"

"I'm pretty sure you were thinking, 'Wow, this feels fucking amazing,' " Preston says as he flips their positions and reaches down to unzip his own fly. "Now how about returning the favor?"

Unable to make eye contact, Scott is pulling up his pants and trying to remember how to get home. "Sorry… I can't. I shouldn't have let this happen."

"You're not fucking serious, are you?"

Still slightly out of breath, Scott rakes a hand through his hair. He knows he's being unfair; he should have put on the brakes, but Preston had been so insistent, and he'd just been so turned on.

Scott tries putting on his best contrite smile. "I'm really sorry, Preston. This just isn't me; I don't usually do this."

"Christ, you're a fucking tease, just like Jamie," Preston says, pushing off from the door and pointing at Scott. "Actually no, you're worse."

"What are you talking about?" Scott asks, standing up straight and tucking his shirt back into his pants.

"At least he put out first!"

"He… what?" Scott stammers. Preston must find the look of shock on his face amusing because he laughs.

"Oh yeah," he says. "Jamie was a fantastic fuck. Not much of a talker, but he made these delicious noises, all gasps and whimpers and, 'Fuck me harder, Preston.'"

Preston's voice pitches higher as he mimics gasps and moans. Scott's face flushes hot and his hands clench in fists.

"Then of course he had to go and fuck everything up by getting all clingy and shit."

"What the *fuck* are you talking about?" Scott demands. His mind flashes back to a text message from a few weeks ago when Jamie apologized for being a clingy drunk, but nothing could be further from the truth. If anything, Jamie goes out of his way *not* to touch people. Scott's brain cannot reconcile his version of Jamie with what Preston is saying.

"I. Fucked. Him. And he loved it. But of course he couldn't just be happy with epic sex. He wanted a fucking *boyfriend*." Preston's lips curl up as if he's just said the most vulgar word in the English language.

"So you just fucked him and then told him to get lost," Scott says through clenched teeth. His eyes are burning, but he'll be damned if he's going to cry in front of this asshole.

"Well I sure as hell wasn't going to play house with him," Preston says, laughing. "He was hot, and his attitude made him a challenge. I had no idea he'd turn out to be so good in bed. I thought we had a good thing going. We'd go out dancing, get drunk, come back here and fuck. When he told that man-child David we were dating, I had to set the record straight."

"How long did that go on?" Scott asks.

"A few weeks maybe," Preston says with a shrug. "I don't know. It was almost a year ago now. Does it matter?"

Scott's heartbeat quickens as he considers this new information. Jamie doesn't date industry people because of Preston; it all makes sense now.

"No," he says, because it doesn't matter—not the way he had thought it would.

"Look, I'm sorry," Preston says, his face softening. He brings a hand up to Scott's shoulder and strokes his thumb slowly over the fabric of Scott's shirt. The gesture isn't threatening, but Scott still tenses. Preston either doesn't notice or chooses to ignore it. "I get kind of pushy when I've been drinking. You don't have to do anything if you don't want to."

Scott's face feels numb. He's completely sober now and just wants to get the hell out of Preston's apartment.

"I think I'm just going to go," he says. His voice sounds strained and deeper than usual.

"You want me to call you a cab?"

"No thanks," Scott says, refusing to make eye contact. "I think I'm going to walk."

When he closes the door behind him, he sags to the floor in the hallway.

* * *

The next morning Scott gets up early. He showers and shaves, puts on his favorite Oxford shirt and his best-fitting jeans. He heads to the deli on the corner, which has the best homemade chicken soup. He buys a quart, along with a delicious, chewy-crusted baguette.

He stops at a florist down the block and buys a bouquet of circus roses—the drama of the bright yellow blooms with deep crimson at the edges seems perfect for the occasion.

He walks into a small, two-story building and knocks on the door of the first apartment. He hears shuffling inside and a voice calls out, "Just a minute!"

While he waits, Scott hums to himself, a tune he's had stuck in his head since his shower, until the door is wrenched open almost violently. A pretty girl with shockingly pink hair and dark brown eyes glares at Scott. She must be one of Jamie's roommates.

"Can I help you?" she says.

"I'm looking for Jamie," Scott replies, the sentence coming out more like a question than a definitive statement.

"Hey, Black Plague, you've got a visitor!" she yells, angling her face into the apartment.

"Who is it?" Jamie calls. His voice sounds muffled and hoarse.

"I don't know, some dude with roses. Get off your ass and find out for yourself. I'm late for work!"

"Fine, leave me in my hour of need, " Jamie says, his voice cracking on the last word. He coughs loudly before adding, "Never mind that I'm hacking up a lung, Jules. You go on to work."

"God, he's a fucking drama queen," she says. "Just go on in. I'm sure he'll be out in a minute. If not, his room's the first door on the left."

She steps back to let Scott past her, pulls the door shut and is gone in a whirl of pink hair and black leather. In her wake, Scott takes in the small living room. It's sparsely decorated with mismatched furniture, but still manages to feel like a home. There are framed photos of Jamie with various groups of girls, including the woman who answered the door—with light brown hair instead of pink—on a small bookshelf in the corner, next to a comfy-looking chair and an antique lamp. The sofa looks as if it's had more than one owner, but it's clean and fits well with the décor despite being a crazy '70s floral pattern in varying shades of red and orange. He's admiring a large wall clock that looks like an overgrown stopwatch when he hears a muffled cough from behind him. He turns just as Jamie recognizes him and his eyes go wide.

"Scott!"

"Hi, Jamie," he says with a smile.

"What are you doing here?" he asks, tugging his hoodie closer to his body.

"I heard you were sick. Thought you could use some soup." He holds up the bag from the deli.

Jamie's eyes dart to the bag and then the flowers in Scott's other hand.

"Also for you," Scott says, holding them out. "My nana always liked fresh flowers when she was sick. She said the bright colors took the fever away."

When Jamie steps forward to take the bouquet from him, Scott notices for the first time how puffy and red Jamie's eyes are. His skin has lost its usual pink undertones, his thick auburn hair wild and sticking out in all directions. It's adorable.

"How are you feeling?" Scott asks, following Jamie into the small, bright kitchen.

"Like death," Jamie says. "My fever broke last night, though. So I should be back at work soon."

Scott sets the soup on the counter and pulls out a stool at the island. "Jamie, why don't you sit down, and I'll put those in some water."

Jamie doesn't argue and takes a seat. He folds his arms on the counter and drops his head to rest on them. Scott finds a bowl in one of the cupboards and pours some soup, then searches through drawers until he finds a spoon.

"Here, eat this," he says, nudging it toward Jamie's elbow.

Jamie lifts his head and groans. "God, that smells amazing," he says. "I feel like I haven't eaten in days."

Scott sees a vase on top of the refrigerator and fills it with water, unwraps the roses and places them in it. "There, doesn't that look festive?" His smile feels brighter than the occasion calls for, and he looks expectantly at Jamie, hoping for a reprieve.

"Scott, why are you here?" Jamie asks, spoon halfway to his mouth.

Scott's smile dims as he considers his reasons.

"Because you were right."

"About?"

"Preston. He's a jerk."

"That's an understatement," Jamie says, rolling his eyes.

"And I wanted us to be friends again," Scott says.

"We are friends," Jamie insists.

"You wouldn't return my calls."

"I'm sick."

"Or texts."

"Fine," Jamie says, pouting a little, as if conceding is the last thing he wants to do. "I was a little angry. But I'm not now ... promise."

Scott searches Jamie's face, deciding the slightly pinched, stern look is a result of his illness and not insincerity. Jamie's green eyes shine as he holds Scott's gaze.

They stay like that for a moment, just smiling at each other, both of them reveling in the ease of simply being together. Much like riding a bike or making boxed macaroni and cheese, it's just something they do, as though it's something they've always done. No deep thought or analysis required. And it just feels right.

Jamie blinks slowly and yawns, pulling Scott out of the moment.

"You look tired," Scott says. "Do you need to lie down?"

Jamie shakes his head and swallows a mouthful of soup. "No, I've been doing nothing but sleeping for the last two weeks," he says. "Can you stay for a bit? Maybe we could watch a movie or something?"

"Sure. I'd like that."

Scott doesn't really pay attention to the movie—some drama about young lovers being separated, and the heroine dying of cancer before her lover can tell her how he feels. It's depressing, but Jamie is beautiful as he quietly lets the tears spill, sniffling and coughing periodically from his lingering cold. Scott steals glances, memorizing the pattern of the faint stubble along Jamie's neck and jaw, the way he licks and bites his bottom lip absently. Jamie's lashes are damp and he blinks slowly and dabs at his eyes.

"It's just so sad, you know," Jamie says, sniffling as the credits roll. "She thought he ran off with her best friend, but he got in that car accident, and then when he came back she was already sick. But she didn't want to tell him she was dying, and he thought she didn't love him. And, *God*, when she died, he found those letters."

Scott tries to remember the plot of the movie; he remembers crying and yelling, the beep of a heart monitor … but mostly he remembers Jamie. He laughs at something and Scott glances over at him again. His eyes are gleaming and his cheeks flushing pink.

"You probably think I'm being silly," he says.

"Nothing silly about being a romantic."

Scott looks at Jamie, *really* looks at him, rumpled and un-showered, sniffling and crying, dressed in sweat pants and an old T-shirt and hoodie, and realizes he's fallen in love. In spite of all the insistence on being friends and the ten-year age difference, he's completely gone. Jamie is what he wants.

"Jamie…" Scott inhales around the word; it comes out barely a sound, choked and emotional.

"My mom has cancer," Jamie says suddenly.

Scott blinks at him, unsure if he's heard him correctly.

"Your m– I'm sorry… cancer?"

"Breast cancer. She had surgery last month," Jamie says. "She's fine now, mostly. Gets tired easily. But you know I told you my dad had a heart attack a few years ago, and sometimes I'm just scared that something is going to happen and I'll lose someone else I care about."

"Does your family still live in Missouri?"

"My mom does, with my stepdad, Alan, and his son, Jake," he says. "My sister, Maisie, lives in LA. She said she wanted some sunshine in her life after all that pain." A smile tilts the corners of his mouth when he mentions her.

"When was the last time you went home?"

"Um, last Christmas, I think. It's been a while."

"Maybe you need to plan a trip," Scott suggests. Just because he's not close with his parents, it doesn't mean he can't understand the concept. He finds himself feeling a little jealous of Jamie and immediately chastises himself. Jamie's mom is sick.

"I don't even know why I'm telling you all this," Jamie says. "I don't …" He pauses, grabbing a tissue to wipe his nose. "I don't talk about this stuff often."

"Why not?"

"I just… don't," he says with a shrug. "No one to tell."

For a brief second, Scott considers confessing his feelings to Jamie, unloading it all, but he senses now isn't the time. Besides, he needs more time to figure it out for himself, and their friendship is more important to him than his own feelings at the moment. He needs to let Jamie know that. Reaching out to rest his hand on Jamie's tense back, Scott begins rubbing loose circles; eventually he feels the muscles begin to relax. No, now is not the time to unload his feelings for Jamie or his guilt for going out with Preston.

"Well, now you have me," Scott says, smiling, hoping Jamie understands how much he means it.

Chapter 8

It's almost evening by the time Scott gets home, and he's completely exhausted. Planning to take a long nap and a hot shower, he's greeted by an overly inquisitive Ben who's obviously had a full night's sleep and, from the smell of it, has been experimenting with bacon in the kitchen again.

"Out all night?" he asks cheerfully, the second Scott walks through the door. "Must have been some date." He winks cartoon-ishly and walks back into the kitchen.

"For your information, I slept here last night. I just got up early to take Jamie some soup because he's sick. But thanks for being a predictable perv."

"What's up your ass?" Ben snaps as he returns with a plateful of bacon and avocado pizza. "Or is it what *isn't* up your ass that's the problem?"

"Sometimes you can be a real bag of dicks, Ben, you know that?"

He sets the plate down on the coffee table and pats Scott on the back. "Easy, man, it was just a joke. Everything okay?"

Scott sags onto the couch and drops his head on the back of it, staring up at the ceiling. "Yes and no."

"You're going to have to clarify a bit," Ben says, easing down next to him.

"I got a blow job." *And I'm in love with one of my best friends,* he adds mentally.

"What's wrong with that?"

"It was Preston." Scott takes a deep breath and closes his eyes. "He got pissed because I wouldn't return the favor."

Ben lets out a slow whistle. "Not cool, man."

"I was drunk," Scott adds. "It was a mistake."

"Been there."

"You got a blowjob from a guy and refused to reciprocate?" Scott says with a sardonic laugh.

Ben slaps him on the leg. "You know what I mean," he says, picking up his pizza and taking a humongous bite. A piece of avocado falls in his lap, and he picks it up and shoves it in with the rest of his mouthful. Between bites he asks, "So are you going to tell Jamie?"

"To be honest, I don't know," Scott replies. "It's not like it's going to happen again, and I don't want Jamie to find out, but I don't want to lie to him about it either."

"Well, it's not exactly a lie if you just fail to mention it."

"Not helpful," Scott says, his head now throbbing as he considers skipping the shower and going straight to bed.

Ben wipes a smear of marinara sauce off his chin with the back of his hand. "Why don't you want to tell him?"

"He and Preston have a history, and I don't want him to get hurt." Scott looks down at his shoes. Is that really the only reason, he wonders.

"So it has nothing to do with the fact that Jamie has a thing for you?" Ben asks.

"We're just friends. How many times do I have to tell you that?"

"Until it's the truth," Ben replies smugly before standing and sauntering back to the kitchen with his plate.

Scott gets up and follows him. "You think I'm lying?"

Ben drops his plate in the sink without rinsing it and turns to face him. "Look, I know you've convinced yourself that you're 'just friends' with this guy, but I think it's time you did some soul searching, dude."

"Ben, I know this may surprise you, but not all gay men are dying to get into each other's pants."

"Maybe not, but are you actually going to stand there and tell me you don't have feelings for Jamie? Because from where I stand, you're fucking head over heels for the guy and just too damned stubborn to admit it."

Ben's words hit Scott like a punch to the gut. He reaches behind him and sits down on one of their kitchen chairs and begins to mentally catalogue the entirety of his relationship with Jamie. "Is it that obvious?"

"Only to people with eyes."

"Holy shit," he says.

"And there it is," Ben says, nodding his head and gloating.

"Do you think Jamie knows?"

"It depends," Ben says with a shrug. "Is he as stubborn and willfully blind as you?"

"I'm serious, Ben. He's still hung up on Preston, and I'm really trying to be a good friend here. I can't tell him how I feel. Not yet. It would ruin everything."

"So you're just going to keep playing this 'friends' angle?"

"It's not an angle," Scott says. "We're friends."

"But you have feelings for him."

Scott looks away, focusing on the geometric pattern of their kitchen linoleum. "I think I might be in love with him," he says.

"Shit, son. You're fucked."

* * *

The photo shoot the following week sneaks up on him, giving Scott little time to prepare himself for how he's going to approach the Preston situation at work. Sheena does the work for him.

"So I heard you went on a date with Preston," she says as soon as she sees him.

She's applying makeup to Adamo's neck and trying not to stare at where her assistant is applying sunless tanner to Noel's bared abs. If the furtive glances she's shooting his way every five seconds are any indication, she's losing that battle pretty epically.

"Um, sort of," Scott says, flicking mindlessly through a tray of makeup brushes. He likes Sheena; she's easy to talk to and she listens without offering unsolicited advice. It's refreshing after dealing with Ben's incessant meddling. And Adamo, of course, barely understands a word they're saying.

"Sort of? Either it was a date or it wasn't." She shoots another glance in Noel's direction.

"Well, it was a date at first, but by the end of the night, I was pretty sure I didn't want it to be."

"Oh." She taps Adamo on the left shoulder and asks, "Can you turn to the left for me, sweetie?" He smiles at her, nodding blankly but not moving. "God, if this one knew five words of English, it would make my job so much easier." She nudges him into the position she wants. "At least he's stopped quoting *The Princess Bride* and *Casablanca* at me."

Scott looks up questioningly.

"Earlier, every time I'd ask him a question he'd respond with 'as you wish' or 'here's looking at you, kid.' I thought I was going to pee my pants laughing."

Scott looks at Adamo; he's smiling at Sheena, completely enthralled, taking in every movement she makes and word she speaks. Sheena is practically oblivious to his presence until he says "As you wish" again.

"See?" Sheena giggles and Scott can't help but join her.

"I think someone has a crush on you," he says.

"You're one to talk," Sheena says, her eyes flitting over to Noel again. "Preston looks at you like he hasn't eaten a full meal in days and you're prime rib."

"Nice," Scott says. "Compare me to a piece of meat."

"You know what I mean," she says, maneuvering around Adamo's long legs to get to his left side. His dark eyes follow her the whole time.

"Yeah, and actually it's a pretty accurate assessment of the situation," he says. "But it was just the one date, so if you don't mind, I'd rather it didn't get around."

"Well you probably should tell Preston that," she says.

Scott stands up straighter, his full attention on Sheena as he asks, "What do you mean?"

"He's been bragging to anyone who will listen that you and he had a 'moment.' " The air quotes make evident what he's been implying to their coworkers.

Scott is furious. He can't believe Preston would do that.

"God, that guy is infuriating," Scott says. "Wait… everyone?"

"Just about," she says, glancing up at Scott. "Why?"

"Jesus, Sheena, I don't need the whole crew thinking I slept with him."

"So you didn't?" She looks genuinely shocked.

"Not exactly," Scott says.

"What's that supposed to mean?"

"That's none of your business … or anyone else's," he says.

"Sorry," she says, her look of concern and remorse unmistakable. "I just thought… Well, sometimes things happen, Scott. It's nothing to be ashamed of."

"Well it's never happening again."

Scott returns his attention to the brushes, flicking through them forcefully.

"Why not?" she asks, raising her eyebrows dramatically. "He's cute."

Scott rolls his eyes. "As if that's the only requirement for having sex."

"What about Jamie?" she asks so quietly that only Scott can hear.

"What *about* Jamie?"

He's not sure if Sheena is asking about *his* relationship with Jamie or if she knows about Jamie's past with Preston, but he doesn't get a chance to ask. Jamie walks in at that very moment, sporting a new scarf and looking as if he'd never been sick.

"Yeah, what about me?"

Scott's gaze shoots back to Sheena at the sound of Jamie's voice, his heart racing. He wants to crawl under the floorboards.

"Jamie!" he says, a little too exuberantly and smiling too widely as he turns to face him. After Scott's visit to Jamie's apartment, he knew he didn't want to tell Jamie he went out with Preston because it's not happening again. It was a one-time thing. But faced with the prospect of telling Jamie about it at all, he's not sure if that's the right choice. He's not sure there is a right choice.

"Oh, we were just talking about the shoot," Sheena says, barely looking up from her work on Adamo. "Scott here—"

"Needs to go help Zach get set up," Scott interrupts, grateful for the chance to escape the conversation. "See you out there, Jamie. Thanks, Sheena."

As Scott leaves, he hears Sheena artfully change the subject. He knew there was a reason he liked working with her.

"So, Jamie," she says. "I heard you booked another campaign… big client too."

"Maybe," he says. "I may not take it."

Jamie's voice fades as Scott turns back to the open area of the loft. He is so busy straining to hear Sheena and Jamie's conversation that he doesn't notice Preston heading his direction until he's right on top of him.

"Hey, sexy," Preston says, running a hand up Scott's arm.

Scott shrugs it off, gritting his teeth as he asks, "What are you telling everyone about our date?"

"I didn't tell *everyone*," Preston says. "I only mentioned it to Zach. He asked me about my weekend."

"And you felt the need to imply that something happened between us?"

"Well, it did." He leans in and waggles his eyebrows at Scott, trying to look flirtatious; it just looks ridiculous to Scott, and he jabs a finger into Preston's chest.

"Look, Preston, I'd appreciate if if you'd stop running your mouth about my personal life to my crew."

"Jesus," he says, backing away. "Sorry, Scott. I was just joking around a little. You don't have to be so touchy. But maybe you should talk to *your* crew about not gossiping behind your back." He backs away from Scott before heading to hair and makeup.

Scott looks over Preston's shoulder and sees Jamie staring at him, mouth agape. Jamie's eyes flit from Scott to Preston and his face clouds over before his expression is completely closed off. It appears Jamie has built up the wall between himself and Scott all over again.

Scott can't face it. Storming out of the room, he tries his best to focus on his work. Fury propels him through the day and leaves him feeling as if he's in a fog; back to square one with the entire crew, not knowing what to say to anyone, especially Jamie. He's not really directing the models or helping Zach, but he can't help it; everything feels off.

Only Preston remains unchanged, dropping innuendo and flirting blatantly.

The day gets stranger still when Jamie starts his own flirting—with Adamo of all people. At first, Scott isn't sure if it's actually happening or if he's imagining it, because it starts out subtly. Jamie laughs a little too loudly at something Adamo says. Later, he puts a hand on Adamo's knee when Sheena touches up his makeup, ignoring the smitten look Adamo is shooting in Sheena's direction.

"Adamo," Jamie says, running a hand along his arm after Sheena walks away, "you should get me the number for your trainer."

Scott rolls his eyes. This is getting ridiculous. Jamie's obviously trying to make a point to Preston, who's only standing two feet away, but Scott knows Preston's not interested in Jamie, and he can't stand to see Jamie get hurt by Preston again.

Despite his best efforts to get Jamie's attention, Scott's only chance to talk to him is during their lunch break. As usual, most of the crew and the models are chatting and enjoying a few moments off their feet. Jamie is by himself, eyes glued to his phone. He doesn't even look up when Scott approaches.

"Jamie, why are you doing this?"

"I have to get back to the agency about my next job," he says. "I didn't realize it was a crime to have lunch alone."

"That's not what I meant, and you know it," Scott half whispers through gritted teeth.

Jamie's mouth curls into a sneer, his jaw set. "I'm afraid you're going to have to spell it out for me," he says. "Us dumb models aren't really that quick, you know."

Scott feels his frustration fading once he realizes he's obviously hit a nerve. He doesn't want to pick a fight with Jamie. He just wants to protect him from being hurt by Preston again.

"Jamie, come on. You know I don't think that, and besides, I'm talking about the over-the-top flirting with Adamo."

"What do you care?"

"Well, he's straight for one," Scott says. "And two, it's like you're *hate* flirting. Will you just tell me what's wrong?"

Jamie looks down at his hands, threading his fingers together and fidgeting. His furious expression begins to fade, but he doesn't look up.

When he doesn't answer, Scott softens his tone and leans down into Jamie's line of sight. "Is it because of Preston?"

Eyes flashing with shock and humiliation, Jamie looks up at Scott. As his eyes start to well up, Scott sees his upper lip quiver. Maybe he'd underestimated Jamie's feelings for Preston. He's clearly still hung up on the guy. Scott needs to make this easier on him, let Jamie know that he knows.

"Preston doesn't mean anything to me," he says, reaching out to touch Jamie's shoulder. "And even if I were interested in him, I wouldn't go after someone a friend had feelings for."

Jamie jerks away. "Oh my God … *really*?"

"What?" Scott has no idea what he's said. Jamie has to know how obvious his feelings are.

"I'm not interested in Preston!" he shouts. A few heads turn in their direction, and Jamie blushes. He grabs Scott by the arm and drags him into the hair and makeup room.

"Jamie, I don't understand," Scott says once Jamie has shut the door behind them. "If this isn't about Preston, what's going on?"

Jamie shuffles his feet, and looks at a spot over Scott's head, fighting back tears. "I *know*," he says.

"Know what?" Scott asks. He has no idea what Jamie is talking about and he really wishes Jamie would just spit it out because he's starting to get a headache.

"I know that you went on a date with Preston."

"Oh."

"Yeah… oh," Jamie says, looking defeated. "*God*, I feel so stupid. He was going on and on about how you went back to his place and that he can't wait to take you out again and how great your ass is…"

"He said all that?"

Jamie's eyes narrow as he finally meets Scott's gaze. There's something he's not understanding , but he can't quite read between the lines. He tries to explain himself anyway.

"Jamie, I'm really not interested in him. We went on one date. That's all. I swear."

"Why couldn't you just tell me that then? I had to hear about it from fucking Preston of all people! Talking about you like you were some sort of prize he'd won!"

"I think I can handle a little gossip," Scott says, trying to reassure himself as much as Jamie. "I didn't even know about your past with him until the other night. If I had known, I would have never—"

"But it's *Preston*," Jamie says, as if that explains everything. "And, of course, he fucking told you about us."

"Look, I just wanted to go out and have a good time. I'm not going out with him again."

"Well, Preston has no problem showing anyone a good time," Jamie scoffs.

"I know he's a prick, but give the guy a break," Scott says. "I don't think he knows how to have a boyfriend."

"Well, that's abundantly clear," he scoffs. "So what, you thought you'd just get an easy fuck out of him and go back to being my friend?"

"Jesus, Jamie, I didn't fuck him. I was lonely; he asked me to dinner, and I said yes. What was I supposed to do? I've been so busy trying to be your friend that I've blown off all my other friends, and I spent my fucking birthday alone!"

"How is that my fault?" Jamie shrieks.

"You could have at least texted me!"

Jamie reels, and Scott instantly regrets his words. There's no way Jamie knew Scott was alone on his birthday, and it's not his job to make sure Scott stays entertained.

"I didn't even know it was your birthday!" he says. "And besides…"

"Besides what?"

Jamie opens his mouth as if he's got something else to say, but he clamps it shut just as quickly. He throws his head back in exasperation and sighs. "You wouldn't understand."

"Then tell me." Scott doesn't even try to conceal the pleading tone in his voice. When he makes eye contact with Jamie, he smiles, willing Jamie to go on. He hates to see him in such pain. "I'm your friend, remember?" he says after a moment. Jamie's face falls.

"Just forget it," Jamie says, waving him off. "Our lunch break is almost over. Let's get back to work."

"Hey," Scott says, grabbing his arm gently. "I'm the art director. I think everyone will understand. Now talk to me."

"You're right," Jamie says, jerking his chin up. "*You're* the art director." He tugs his arm out of Scott's tentative grip and wheels around on him. "You know, you wouldn't even have this stupid job if it wasn't for me!"

"What's that supposed to mean?"

Scott knows his success with Jamie at the first shoot was largely thanks to Jamie's ability to know his angles, but he'd directed that shoot *and* edited the photos. It's not as though Jamie did all the work.

"Nothing. It means nothing," Jamie says, sounding calmer. "I hope you enjoy dating Preston." He gives Scott a forced smile, and then he's gone.

"But I'm not dating Preston," Scott says to the empty room.

He stands there, wondering what vital piece of information he's missed. Jamie's behavior doesn't match his words, and Scott is more confused than ever. Not only that, he thought they'd made some significant strides at Jamie's apartment the other day, but now Scott's not so sure.

Scott has struggled to keep his true feelings hidden so that his burgeoning friendship with Jamie could remain intact, and he's failed at every turn. Jamie seems to feel betrayed, and who can blame him? Scott hooked up with a guy who'd hurt him and for whom he still has feelings. Scott's certain of that, no matter what Jamie says.

Scott realizes that he has to live with the fact that he's fallen in love with someone—someone who's still in love with another man. The realization hurts.

Why does it have to be Preston of all people? Even though Scott thinks that, deep down, Preston's probably not as bad as everyone suspects, he knows he has broken Jamie's heart once already, and now Scott has wounded Jamie's pride. Some friend.

He takes a few deep breaths and opens the door to the loft. He hears a shrill voice call out, "Where in God's name is the fucking art director?"

He'd know that voice anywhere. It's Jan West. What is the client doing on set? He ducks behind a support beam and grabs his phone to call Lorelei.

"Hello, Ms. West, I'm Jamie Donovan." Scott can just barely make out Jamie's voice from where he's hiding. He leans forward to get a better look.

"You're Donovan?" she says, a perfectly arched eyebrow raised in question.

"Yes."

"You're too short," she says curtly, dismissing him with a single wave. "Would someone please tell me where the fucking art director is?"

Chapter 9

Jan West towers over Scott in her three-inch heels—conservative in the fashion world, but at nearly six feet tall, she doesn't need the boost—making quite a scene dressed in head-to-toe black, her silver-white hair pinned back in a tight chignon. She reminds Scott of his paternal grandmother—prickles and ice and no trace of warmth.

Grandmother Parker came from old money and made it clear she'd never approved of her son's decision to marry someone outside their pretentious inner circle of New England WASPs. She directed a lot of her disdain for Scott's mother at Scott, perhaps because he'd been unfortunate enough not to inherit the Parker height or stunning blue eyes. His brother Chris had gotten both, whereas Scott favored his mother.

He takes a deep breath and pockets his phone; Lorelei will have to wait. If he's already lost this account, he'd rather get a chance to clear out his desk and say goodbye to Yvonne before Lorelei fires him.

Scott puts on his best smile and squares his shoulders, falling back on his prep school upbringing and all those years of his mother telling him to sit up straight, as he approaches his client. "Ms. West, Lorelei didn't tell me you'd be coming by today," Scott says, holding out a hand for her to take. "What a pleasant surprise."

Jan West's blue eyes pierce through Scott as if he's made of straw, a sad sack of a brainless oaf, which Scott thinks might be pretty accurate at this point. He can't even manage to keep from hurting his best friend for more than five minutes at a time. Standing next to a force of nature like Jan West, Scott has never felt quite so small or childlike. A former model, she's taller than everyone in the loft, except for Preston and Adamo. How had Jamie just walked up to her? Scott never would have taken the initiative if Jan hadn't sought him out. Well, screamed for him, to be precise.

Scott looks up expectantly, hand still extended.

"That's because she doesn't know I'm here," Jan says, looking down her nose at Scott as if she refuses to lower her head, or herself, to his level. "And you are?"

"Oh, I'm sorry," he says, pulling his hand back abruptly. "Scott Parker. I'm the art director for your holiday campaign."

She sniffs. "*This* model is too short," she says waving a hand at Jamie. She doesn't even look at him. "We need to reshoot."

Jamie is shooting daggers at Jan with his eyes; the similarity between the two when they're judging someone is uncanny. Scott wonders if Jamie realizes it or if it's one of those situations where you hate someone because subconsciously they remind you of the things you hate most about yourself.

Jan strides over to the rack of clothes where Isaac is working and starts rearranging his styling. Scott sees him tense as she destroys hours of work in a matter of seconds.

"Don't you think that's a little rash?" Scott asks, approaching her cautiously. He's not quite sure if he means reshooting or restyling, maybe both.

Jan turns and looks at him, hand frozen in mid air with a silk tie between her bony fingers. She's looking at Scott as if he's just suggested she wear off-the-rack.

"I was clear about the height requirements for my models, was I not?" she asks.

"You definitely were," Scott says, "but I think if you—"

"So my instructions were clear, but you chose to ignore them?"

"Not at all Ms. West, but I thought you might like to see what we've been shooting," he says. "I think you'll agree that Jamie is exactly the right model for the One West line."

"You think I don't know my own style, Matt?"

Scott resists the urge to correct her as he tries to remain diplomatic. "I just think if you saw what we've been working on, you'd see that we're going for something edgier, something that I think will wipe the floor with the competition. You'll be the name on everyone's lips next season."

She narrows her eyes and says, "You have that much confidence in your work, do you?"

Scott nods. "I do."

"That kind of arrogance will either get you promoted or fired," she says.

The two stare at each other for a moment, Scott worrying that his fate will be the latter, when she says, "Okay, wow me."

Scott claps his hands sharply and glances around frantically, trying to remember where he'd left his laptop. He spots it next to Zach's camera bag and opens it, their last hundred or so frames still on the screen. He pulls up the group shots, thinking he stands his best chance if he can show how they managed to mask Jamie's height next to the much-taller models.

"So what we're going for here is this twist on the urban chic thing—"

"Isn't that kind of overdone?" she asks.

"Exactly," Scott says. "Which means that all the other designers will be going in a completely opposite direction. So we thought, let's take urban chic and turn it on its ear. Why not contrast the edginess of your line against a rural backdrop and then intersperse that with this more whimsical, but slightly stark style?" He clicks through a few shots from the shot at the lake and then shows her some of the stuff they've shot today. "See how the two styles play off each other and the garments just pop?"

He doesn't mention the models, even though they were chosen for their eclectic looks too. The deep brown of David's skin next to Jamie's fair complexion provides a sharp contrast for the lake shots, while Preston's lanky, muscular build and Noel's chiseled physique set off the sharp angles of Jamie's thinner frame. David's body type is different still, and in each shot there's something to draw the eyes. Scott hadn't realized just what great work they were doing. He's proud of it.

He looks up at Jan expectantly.

"This one is still too short." She points to Preston, though.

Scott bites his lip to keep from correcting her. He looks over at where Jamie and the other models are standing, fascinated by the scene unfolding before them.

"It's all part of the concept," Scott says, his confidence waning. "I promise you, it will all come together and you're going to love it."

"And if I don't?" she asks, skeptical.

"Then Price will reshoot the entire campaign for free." He's taking a big risk, but there's no way he's backing off from this idea now. Scott believes in it. It's strong, and Jamie is the perfect model for this line—the embodiment of urban chic with a twist of whimsy. What's more, the group shots are some of the best work he's ever seen from Zach, and it's a fresh concept.

"You've got balls, kid," she says, a tight, clipped smile on her face.

Scott lights up. "I promise you," he says. "This campaign will blow your mind."

"It had better," she says, standing up and flipping her scarf over her shoulder. "Don't tell Lorelei I came by. She'll get all antsy and start calling me every day to see if I'm happy. I can't stand that."

"No problem," Scott says.

She nods curtly, slipping her large Dior sunglasses over her nose. She makes a noncommittal "mmm" sound, and then, almost as quickly as she'd come, she's gone.

Her exit reminds Scott of a ridiculous cross between Miranda Priestly from *The Devil Wears Prada* and the Dowager Countess of Grantham. He bites back his laughter as he turns to face his astonished crew.

Isaac looks as if he's ready to cry, taking in the mess Jan made of the clothing racks; Zach is grinning at Scott. The models stand nearby, slack-jawed and confused, especially Adamo. All except Jamie, whose expression is unreadable.

Scott claps his hands to get their attention. "All right, people— let's get to work."

* * *

Scott takes a seat in the coffee shop he's come to think of as his and Jamie's, even though they haven't met here in weeks. He taps his foot as he waits for Jamie to arrive; he's twenty minutes late already, and Scott's starting to think he's backed out.

Jamie had wanted to meet up for coffee and talk about things, but he'd been pretty vague when Scott had pressed for more information, insisting that Scott should meet him at their usual place at the usual time.

Scott is nursing his second cup of coffee, never more thankful that he doesn't drink espresso; he's already jittery as his mind works overtime trying to figure out what Jamie wants to talk about. Unable to piece together a coherent thought on the matter, he swirls the dregs of his coffee, noting a few grounds in the bottom of the cup mixed with some undissolved sugar crystals. This place doesn't even have particularly good coffee, but he's contemplating a third cup anyway. Just as he glances toward the line at the counter, Jamie walks in.

No, not walks, glides. Drifts? Floats? None of those words do justice to the way Jamie looks stepping through the door of the coffee shop. In all the excitement at work, Scott had forgotten how utterly magnificent Jamie is. Transfixed by the sight before him—a vision in leather, cotton and silk—Scott feels his stomach bottom out, like going over the first drop on a roller coaster. Similarly, there's no going back in his relationsip with Jamie, he realizes suddenly. He's going over that hill now whether he wants to or not. The question is, how big is the drop and is Jamie up for the ride too? The idea makes him feel shaky and weak, and also a little bit thrilled.

"Hi," Jamie says, sounding out of breath and pretty much perfect. "Sorry I'm late. I almost got tackled by one of those bike messengers on my way over here and stumbled into some lady who couldn't be bothered to put a lid on her latte. So I had to rush home and change. I'm pretty sure the vest I was wearing is ruined. Thank God it was from a sample sale."

"It's okay," Scott says, already feeling more at ease in the wake of Jamie's cute, nervous rambling. "I got caught up on emails while I was waiting." He presents his phone as evidence of his lie, wiggling it around as if that might make it true.

Jamie smiles at him and says, "Good, then I don't feel as bad. Did you need a refill? I'm going to go grab something."

Scott nods and hands Jamie his cup. "Thanks."

"Still stuck on that horrible drip coffee, I see."

"I like the drip coffee."

"Old man."

Scott shrugs. "I like what I like."

There's easy affection in their banter; it calms Scott's nerves even further, and he's grateful. Perhaps Jamie is ready to move on from their argument after all. However, when Jamie returns with their coffee, his mood is somber, as though he's had time to think about what he wants to say, and it's not good. Scott braces himself for the impact of Jamie's words.

"I wanted to thank you for defending me to Jan West," Jamie says. "You didn't have to do that… especially after I yelled at you."

Scott exhales in a rush of breath, relieved that Jamie isn't angry. "It's my job," he says, shrugging it off as if that's the only reason he did it.

"It's your job to please the client," Jamie corrects. He purses his lips and looks thoughtful. "Did you mean it?"

"That you're the right look for the campaign? Yeah, I meant it. You're the best model we have on One West. Hands down."

Jamie looks as though he doesn't quite believe him. "Well, I can't help but be fabulous." He laughs.

Scott reaches across the table and puts his hand over Jamie's. The sudden contact startles Jamie and he tries to pull back, but Scott stops him.

"No, it's more than that, Jamie. You're so talented, and I think this job could be the jumping off point for your career. I bet everyone is talking about you come December."

Scott moves his hand away and leans back, watching Jamie, something unreadable in his features.

"Maybe." Jamie takes a drink of his chai and looks out the window for a moment, his eyes following a woman in a billowing green sundress. When she passes out of view, he turns back to Scott. "Do you really think I'm talented?"

"Definitely."

"Thanks," he says softly, his hands toying with his cup again. He suddenly straightens up. "And it's none of my business if you date Preston."

"I'm not *dating* Preston."

"Still—"

"I'm not," Scott says, trying to reassure him with his eyes. "It was one date, and I'm not interested."

Jamie leans toward Scott, holding out his hand tentatively. Scott looks down at Jamie's outstretched hand—his slightly curved palm, long and slender fingers, perfectly manicured nails—and then back up at Jamie questioningly. The warm smile on Jamie's face urges him on, so he takes Jamie's hand and squeezes. It's a friendly gesture, Scott thinks, nothing more, but he can't help but consider that Jamie has somehow let him back in, and it feels really, really good.

"Okay," Jamie says. "I'm sorry I jumped to conclusions."

Jamie squeezes back and then lets go, turning to look out the window again. Scott takes the opportunity to rest his hand in his lap, flexing his fingers and savoring the lingering warmth from Jamie's touch. He looks at his palm, no different than before, but the sensation lingers, a feeling of belonging and acceptance. Safe. It feels like coming home, to a place he knows he can just... *be*.

So for a moment, he lets himself do just that, reveling in the comfort of Jamie's presence and the background noise of the café until the contrasting silence reminds him of his family and the uncomfortable quiet of the dinner table. He wonders what Jamie's family meals were like. Were they cold, formal affairs like at the Parker home? Or warm, family moments that you want to savor? Probably the latter.

"So, how's your mom?" Scott asks. Maybe he's steering the conversation, but he doesn't want to reveal too much. He can't scare

Jamie off when everything still feels so new, as if it's precariously resting on the head of a pin and could tip over and be lost at any moment.

"Better," Jamie says. "My stepbrother says he'll keep an eye on her for me, go home on weekends more often."

"Good. I'm glad to hear you've got someone you can trust."

"I do," Jamie says, affection in his eyes. He must really be close to his family. Jamie shakes his head a little, just a fraction, but it looks as though he's trying to shake off a stray thought. "I talked to Jake yesterday, actually. He wants to come visit. Says he wants to meet all my 'fancy modeling friends.'" Jamie uses air quotes and laughs. His lips curve into a more intimate smile. "I told him about you."

Scott's swallow of coffee catches in his throat. "What?" he sputters around a cough.

"Yeah, I told him I'd made friends with the art director." Jamie pauses and smiles impishly at Scott. "And then he told me not to piss where I eat." Jamie laughs. "He thought we were dating. Can you believe it?"

Scott shakes his head, eyes wide as he tries to look appropriately shocked, but in reality, he's not sure what to say or how to react.

"But I told him we're just friends," Jamie says. His voice pitches up on the end of the sentence, as if he's asking Scott for clarification, as if he's not quite sure they are friends anymore.

"Of course we're friends." Scott chuckles softly. "I just can't believe he jumped from, 'Hey I made friends with my art director,' to 'Oh, they must be fucking.'"

Jamie laughs, all traces of worry gone from his face. "Well, to be fair, my stepbrother's only examples for gay men are me and that one time we watched *Brokeback Mountain* together."

"*God*, that must have been awkward."

"You have no idea."

"Still, I can't imagine anyone in my family even agreeing to watch that movie, let alone watching it *with* me," Scott says. "You're lucky, Jamie."

"I am," Jamie says. "They're great."

"I hope I get to meet them sometime."

Jamie's eyes go wide and he tilts his head to the side. Scott panics. Did he say the wrong thing? He tries to recover. "I just meant—"

"No, it's okay," Jamie says, reaching out and patting Scott's hand. "You just shocked me that's all. But it's sweet that you'd want to meet my family. I'm sure they'd love to meet you… I— I mean… well, at least Jake said he wanted to meet my friends. So I'm sure—"

"Jamie…" Scott begins. Jamie pauses mid sip and raises an eyebrow. Scott feels that weird swoopy feeling in his gut, like he did the first time Jamie looked at him that way. He exhales a shuddering breath. "I—"

"I think I love you," Jamie says.

"What?" Scott's jaw drops open.

Jamie points up nonchalantly, taking a sip from his chai. "The song, 'I Think I Love You.' The Partridge Family? I can't believe they're playing this."

"Oh yeah … right," Scott says as his heart races in his chest, adrenalin coursing through his veins. "The Partridge Family."

The song is just audible over the din of the coffee shop, and Scott strains to hear it. When he picks up the words, he stifles the urge to sing along with David Cassidy on the chorus as he asks himself what he's so afraid of.

Chapter 10

As the holiday campaign wraps up, and Price is gearing up to focus on One West's spring campaign, Scott finds himself becoming friends with Preston. Well, as much as one can be friends with Preston Worth. Mostly they just exchange the stray text and talk about life under the thumb of old money. Scott got out; Preston's still trying.

Preston is also still trying to get Scott to go out with him again, though with less intensity than before. Scott politely declines his invitations, but he doesn't discourage the interaction. Maybe he feels a little guilty after being so nasty to him. Or maybe he just likes the attention. Scott hasn't really decided.

"So, I was thinking," Preston says. "We should go to that club opening next week. I bet there will be some serious eye candy, and you and I could make quite a team."

Scott is tying Preston's tie while Isaac takes care of an issue with the sizing on Noel's shirt. The dry cleaners had lost a few of the samples—Scott's pretty sure they ruined them and are lying—but Isaac has to make do with what was in stock, and nothing fits.

"Preston, I'm not interested. I told you before—"

"I meant as friends," Preston says, stilling Scott's movements by placing a hand on his wrist. "You can be my wingman."

The thing is, since Scott has admitted to himself that he's fallen for Jamie, he's not really been interested in dating anyone else or even going out in search of casual hookups.

"Come on," Preston says. "It's one teensy little club opening. I'll get you home before sunrise." He tucks a hand under Scott's chin and tilts his head up and pouts at him.

"Please, I haven't gotten laid in two weeks."

Scott laughs. Of course Preston would see that as the end of the world.

"Yeah, okay." Scott says. "I'll go."

* * *

As it turns out, Scott and Preston go out with a group—David, Noel, Sheena, Adamo and Jamie, who also brings his two roommates: Julia, the feisty girl with pink hair who answered the door at Jamie's apartment, and Ashley, an indelible force of sarcasm and humor, whom Scott instantly likes. For some reason, Sheena thinks they should celebrate Scott's birthday, even though they're almost a month late.

They get silly—not drunk, but buzzed and just tipsy enough that it makes their good night even better. Everyone is dancing with everyone in different combinations. Julia finds an athletic-looking redhead in a short skirt and spends at least an hour making out with her on the dance floor. Ben shows up about an hour in, throws back a few shots and challenges David to an arm-wrestling competition. When David wins, Ben sulks for a few moments before finding a petite blonde to dance with.

Sheena pulls out a couple of bottles of nail polish and dares Scott to let her do his nails. He's in such a good mood, he doesn't flinch as she starts painting his nails a deep purple. They're giggling and ridiculous and even Preston isn't behaving too badly, keeping close to Scott's side but flirting with any guy who looks remotely interested.

And then there's Jamie. Scott can sense it; he doesn't need to see the raised eyebrows or tight lips to know that he's fuming.

"You want another drink, Jamie?" Ashley's out of her seat and leaning over the table to get his attention.

"No, thank you," he says, looking utterly miserable.

"Suit yourself," she says, before turning to Adamo and grabbing his hand. "Come on, stud. Let's get you another drink and see if you can teach me some Italian."

A shocked-looking Adamo lets himself be dragged along, and Scott hears Sheena giggle.

"What?" Scott says, turning to her.

"I'm just glad she's taken an interest in Adamo. Noel was getting jealous." She looks over where Noel is standing at the bar, talking to David.

Scott's eyebrows shoot up. Noel and Sheena?

"Yeah, according to Adamo, I'm 'why cave men chiseled on walls.' Can you believe it?" She giggles. "Then Noel told him he was going to chisel his face if he didn't shut up and stop hitting on me. I don't think Adamo had a clue what Noel said to him, but I think he got the gist."

"So you and Noel…"

"He asked me to have dinner with him tomorrow," she says with a shrug and a hint of a knowing smile. "I said yes. Have you seen his abs?"

Scott laughs. "You know I have."

"Well, then you know what I mean," she says, taking a sip of her gin and tonic. "I get all hot and bothered just thinking about it."

"God, doesn't anyone talk about anything other than sex and guys?" Jamie asks. He has his arms crossed over his chest, and a pout that might be funny if his behavior weren't stressing Scott out.

"Sorry, Jamie," Sheena says. "Would you like to talk about something else?"

"No, I'm fine," he says, getting up. "I think I need another drink after all."

Sheena and Scott watch him make his way to the bar.

"He's in a mood," Sheena says.

"Yeah, I think it's because of Preston."

"He knew this was Preston's idea, though, right?"

"Yeah, I just don't think he likes seeing him all over other guys," Scott says.

"Preston?"

Scott nods.

"Scott, can I ask you a question?"

"Sure."

"What's going on with you and Jamie?"

"I told you; we're just friends."

"That may be your intention," she says, "but reality is another matter entirely."

Scott doesn't have a chance to continue their conversation, because Ashley and Jamie have returned from the bar with Adamo in tow.

"I would like to extend to you an invitation to the pants party," Adamo says, his thick accent stilting his words and making Sheena giggle.

Ashley practically cackles. "I've been teaching him new pick up lines," she says.

"So you chose *Anchorman*?" Sheena asks, trying not to laugh.

Ashley shrugs and says, "Sixty percent of the time, it works every time."

They laugh as Adamo looks at them in confusion, his permanently gracious smile plastered to his face. Scott wonders what that's like, never understanding what's going on around you. It takes balls.

"Will someone come dance with me before David realizes my date has gone home and tries to convince me I like dick?" Julia says, glowing and breathless from dancing.

Preston smirks at her. "I'm game. No chance of *me* trying to convert you."

"Stellar," she says. "Let's go, Ralph Lauren." She drags Preston by the wrist to the dance floor.

For all their bickering and name calling, they actually make a good pair. Ashley and Adamo follow, leaving Sheena, Scott, and Jamie to save their table.

"Having fun, Jamie?" Scott asks. Maybe he's poking the bear a little, but he just wants Jamie to cheer up. He doesn't understand what's wrong.

"Yeah, sure… a blast," he says, sneering over his glass.

"I'm going to see if I can find Noel," Sheena says. "You two should talk."

Jamie glares at her, but doesn't say anything.

Scott watches him for a few seconds. Jamie is dressed to the nines, as usual, but he's definitely not himself. "Jamie, is everything all right? Is your mom okay? You seem tense."

"Just peachy," he says, forcing a smile. "I'm fine. My mom's fine. My sister's fine. Everything's fine, Scott. Just drop it."

Scott has his mouth open to say something in response, although he's not sure it would do any good, when Preston returns alone.

"Do you want to dance?" he asks, nodding in Scott's direction. "Jules ditched me for some blonde in a halter top."

"Sounds like a typical Friday night for you," Jamie says.

"You know what, Princess, if you're having such a shit time, why are you here? You're making Scott miserable, and the rest of us are just tolerating you."

"Preston," Scott warns, shaking his head and turning to Jamie. "You're not making me miserable."

"Whatever." Jamie stands up and heads to the bathroom.

When he's out of earshot, Scott turns to Preston. "Could you lay off? Something's up."

"Interesting choice of words," Preston says with a smirk. "Now are you going to dance with me, or not?"

"Not right now," Scott says. His mind is still on Jamie. It's puzzling that he's in such a bad mood; he had been fine earlier at work. Hadn't he? "Maybe later."

As the night wears on, everyone has danced with everyone else in the group. Except Jamie. He's spent the night glaring at them from the table, insisting his new shoes aren't really made for dancing.

Scott keeps turning down Preston's invitations to dance, figuring it's probably best if he keeps this outing on a platonic level, just in case. But he can't help but notice that Preston's exuberance is rubbing off on everyone. It's a great night, and Scott is having fun in spite of Jamie's mood, which has grown progressively more sour with each drink.

Scott returns from the dance floor with Sheena, sweaty and energized. They're still singing along to the last song when they plop down at the table.

"I can't remember the last time I had this much fun," Sheena says.

"Me neither," Scott replies. "God, it's fucking hot in here."

"Feels fine to me," Jamie says.

"That's because you're not dancing," Scott says. He stands up and grabs Jamie by the wrist. "Come on, dance with me." He smiles and waits for Jamie to get up.

"No thank you," he says through gritted teeth.

"Oh, come on… just one teensy little dance?" Scott grins at him, trying to pull Jamie out of his mood. He doesn't like seeing him like this, and since he can't figure out what's wrong, he's just going to try to force him to have a good time.

For a second or two, Jamie looks as if he might say yes, even leans forward a little, and then Preston says, "I'll dance with you." He's standing behind Scott, his timing excellent as always. "That is if Princess Donovan doesn't mind?"

"Why would I mind?" Jamie says, tugging his arm from Scott's hand.

"Well, that's settled then," Preston says, taking Scott's hand.

Scott holds up a finger. "Hang on a second," he says. "Are you sure you don't mind?" he asks Jamie.

"Dance with whoever you want, Scott. Fuck." Jamie throws himself back so forcefully he nearly knocks his chair over, but he recovers quickly, slouching against the smooth wood and crossing his arms while he glares almost petulantly at his drink. "God, I can't believe I let Isaac convince me to be nice to you."

"Isaac?"

"Never mind, just go dance with Preston," he says, nearly spitting out the words.

"I don't even like this song," Scott lies. He doesn't need Jamie to know that he's refusing to dance with Preston because of him.

As if on cue, the song changes.

"Perfect," Preston says. He smiles at Scott and looks to Jamie. "I promise I'll bring him back in one piece."

The look Jamie gives him could cut glass, but Preston seems unfazed. He tugs on Scott's hand and leads them to the dance floor.

Scott reluctantly follows Preston through the crowd, trying not to think about the last time they danced together. He positions himself as far away from Preston as he can and still be dancing *with* him, while angling his body so that he can make out Jamie's hunched shoulders where he's now sitting alone with Sheena.

When he catches Scott looking at him, he turns his eyes back to Sheena as though he's suddenly very interested in something she's saying.

"He'll be alright for a couple of songs," Preston says, leaning into Scott's ear to be heard over the music.

"Who?" Scott tries to act as if he hadn't just been staring at Jamie. Preston's raised eyebrow probably means Scott's a really shitty actor. "I'm just worried about him."

"He'll be fine," Preston insists. "Now can we please dance?"

"We *are* dancing," Scott says.

"You're awfully far away," he says, wrapping an arm around Scott's waist and pulling him closer. "See, that's better."

Preston begins moving his hips with the beat, and Scott finds himself following suit. He loves to dance, and the buzz of the alcohol and the music and atmosphere have put him in the mood. Still, he can't help but notice Jamie's presence. The colored lights and strobes on the dance floor make it difficult to see his expression, but Scott keeps glancing over to make sure he's still there.

Jamie's hunched over a little, studying his own hands; Sheena isn't sitting next to him anymore, and he's alone for the moment. He looks up and catches Scott's eye. Something about it tugs at Scott's heart. He wants to fix whatever pain Jamie is feeling, but he doesn't know how. Jamie won't tell him what's wrong, and everything he's tried tonight has failed. And now, here he is, dancing with Preston, when he'd rather be talking to Jamie.

"Christ, Scott, just go fuck him already," Preston says, twirling Scott out of his arms and disappearing into the mass of bodies gyrating around them.

Scott keeps dancing, though, because when he looks up, Jamie is smiling at him. He gets silly, shaking his ass in Jamie's direction, spinning around and laughing. He motions for Jamie to join him, but Jamie just shakes his head, lifting his straw to his lips and taking a drink. He mimes a toast in Scott's direction.

He shrugs, continuing to dance and spin, winking playfully at Jamie, who's hiding a laugh behind his hand as Ben sits down to join him. *Finally*, Scott thinks. He starts to feel lighter, as though the room has suddenly brightened, the sun coming out after a storm, and then he feels an arm wrap around his waist.

Preston leans close to his ear and says, "Now that's more like it."

As soon as he realizes what's going on, Scott's eyes shoot over to Jamie, but he's up and heading toward the bathroom. As Scott follows, he hears Preston call out, "Go get him, Tiger!"

When Scott finally winds his way through the throng on the dance floor, he finds Jamie standing outside the bathroom door, his head tilted back against the wall as he blinks back tears.

"Someone in there?" he asks as gently and nonchalantly as he can. It's as good a thing to say as anything.

Jamie lets out a humorless laugh, his features immediately twisting back into the same glare he's been aiming at Scott for most of the night, and Scott sees red. He grabs Jamie by his shoulders and shoves him back against the wall, invading Jamie's personal space with his entire body—all five feet, eight inches of him—and pinning Jamie's arms back as he struggles to free himself from Scott's grip.

Scott could let him go. Jamie's not going to run, but Scott has reached his breaking point, and he's over Jamie's fluctuating mood and confusing behavior. This has gone on long enough. They're having this out and they're clearing the air once and for all.

"What is your problem tonight? You've been a total dick to everyone, especially me, and I thought we were friends."

"Well, you're here with that asshole Preston for one," Jamie grits out through clenched teeth. He struggles against Scott's hold again, but Scott only grips him tighter.

"Pres—?" Scott stutters. How is this still an issue? He can almost feel the blood rushing hotter through his veins as his anger flares up. "I told you, I'm not dating Preston. And what does that have to do with you being such a bitch tonight?"

Jamie is glaring at Scott, nostrils flared and jaw tense. But he doesn't speak, which only makes Scott more angry. He pushes his body into Jamie's, pressing him harder against the wall.

"I said, what's your problem with me, Jamie?"

Jamie stares at him for a moment, panting, not quite making eye contact.

"I heard you making plans with him," Jamie says, his teeth clenched and his lips tight. "He said he hadn't gotten laid in weeks and you said okay."

Scott laughs. He can't help it. Jamie's eyes flash in anger and he tries to pull away again, but Scott remains perfectly still, pressing Jamie flush against the wall.

"Jamie, stop," he says. "Just stop. He asked me to be his wingman, and I said yes. Nothing more."

"Just like you were his 'wingman' the night you went out?" Jamie spits.

"What are you talking about?"

"Ben told me Preston gave you a blow job, Scott." The lights shift, casting Jamie in an eerie blue glow. "And you said nothing happened."

"Fuck," Scott says, raking a hand through his sweaty hair.

Jamie's face falls, and tears well up in his eyes. Scott can barely hear him over the music when he says, "So it's true."

"I meant to tell you," he says, "but you were so upset and it was totally irrelevant."

"*Irrelevant*? It's a fucking blow job, Scott. That's not nothing."

"It didn't mean anything. I swear. We're just friends."

"Yeah, that seems to be your M.O.," Jamie scoffs.

"Why are you so upset about it anyway?" Scott asks. He needs to know. He can't keep doing this.

Jamie's breathing picks up, and Scott thinks he's going to answer, but in a split second, everything shifts. Jamie's lips are on his, firm and possessive. It only takes Scott a moment to realize what's happening, and when he does, he responds with his entire body. This is everything he's wanted since he first met Jamie. His hands find the back of Jamie's neck easily as he pulls Jamie closer, and when Jamie's lips part in a gasp, Scott presses in his tongue, desperate for more. The response is immediate; Jamie pushes back and takes control of the kiss, pulling Scott up on his tiptoes as he grips the back of Scott's sweater tightly.

They're kissing. They're pressed up against a wall near a unisex bathroom in a loud, smoke-filled bar, kissing as if they'll never get another chance. It's perfect.

Scott pauses when he hears a giggle to his left—a tall blonde pressing her face into the shoulder of her friend. He and Jamie are blocking the way back to the bar, and the girls are obviously tipsy. Jamie shoves him off, and Scott steps back as the girls pass, giggling the entire time.

Scott can't help but laugh to himself from sheer delight, but when he turns back to Jamie, his face is drawn; he looks pale and panicked.

"We should get back," he says, and races past Scott and out into the noisy bar.

Scott doesn't move for a moment, trying to catch his breath as he comes to terms with what just happened. Jamie kissed him; he kissed Jamie. They kissed.

He actually giggles to himself standing in the small hallway outside the bathroom, his hand clamped over his mouth as his heart races.

He's vaguely aware that Jamie ran off—and they've *got* to talk about this—but he's not letting his mind go there just yet because Jamie kissed him.

God, he feels ridiculous being this giddy over a kiss, but he doesn't care. That kiss was everything, and Scott's been around the block enough to know that not all kisses are the same. Some kisses are just lips and tongues and saliva, a simple matter of putting your face near someone else's and closing the distance between. But other kisses—the kind that you feel in every cell of your body; the ones that make you think you might be the first person in the history of mankind to be kissed; the kind that make you want to write songs in your head while it's happening because if you don't the feeling might fade and you'll forget the adjectives you wanted to use; the kind of kiss he just had with Jamie—well, those kisses are the beginning, the middle, and the end. It's the sort of chemistry, romance and passion people search their whole lives for, and it just happened to Scott. He's not sure what to do with that revelation.

Instead of trying to figure it out, he returns to the table. Jamie is chatting amiably with Ashley as though nothing happened, and Scott just wants to drag him out back and kiss him until they can't breathe. How can he not be reacting to that kiss? Didn't it knock him on his ass too?

"Scott, are you alright?" Sheena asks. "You look white as a sheet."

"Huh? Oh, yeah," Scott says. "I think just maybe… too much dancing?"

"Well sit down and catch your breath," she says, patting the chair between her and Jamie. "Ashley was just telling us about the other phrases she's been teaching Adamo."

Scott sits down and tries to act normal, but he's hyper aware of Jamie's presence: the way his hair is curling slightly near his left ear; the barest hint of stubble along his jaw; how his fingers curl and flex with his movements; how close and full his lips look. He looks different somehow, more complete, as if until now he'd been nothing more than a figment of Scott's imagination, a movie playing in his mind that's now in three dimensions. Scott is dying to talk to him about what just happened. Or maybe not talk at all. He just wants to be alone with him, but it seems Jamie is definitely not having the same problem.

"Can you please teach him that line from *As Good As It Gets*?" Jamie asks Ashley. "I'm dying to hear him impersonate Jack Nicholson with that gorgeous Italian accent of his."

"Which line?"

"You know, when he finally confesses his love to Helen Hunt and he tells her 'You make me want to be a better man.' "

"God, that's a good line," Sheena says.

"I know, right?" Jamie says.

"Oooh, or 'You had me at hello' from *Jerry Maguire*," Sheena says. "I love that line."

"That's such an unromantic movie, though," Jamie replies. "I mean, it's Tom Cruise."

"What's wrong with Tom Cruise?"

"Just, no," Jamie says, shaking his head firmly. "No way."

"Scott, what about you?" Sheena asks. "What romantic movie line do you wish some guy would use on you?"

Scott doesn't even have to think about it. Not really. It's just the first thing that pops into his head. "You should be kissed and often and by someone who knows how," he says. "It's from—"

"*Gone With the Wind*," Sheena says. "Clark Gable says it to Vivien Leigh, and it's probably one of the most romantic movie moments ever. I love that movie so much. Good one, Scott." She sighs fondly.

"Yeah, Jamie and I just saw that at the Trocadero," Scott says. "Remember, Jamie?"

Jamie smiles at him and nods, but doesn't expand on it.

"What about *Casablanca*?" Jamie asks.

"No," Ashley says. "This started because he wouldn't stop trying to talk like Humphrey Bogart. We want him speaking English, not sounding like a film noir character."

"Yeah, I never understood the draw of Bogart," Preston says. "Don't get me wrong, I love *Casablanca*, but how was he ever a sex symbol?"

"This coming from a walking cliché," Jamie quips.

"I thought you'd put the claws away, Pepe Le Pew."

"He was the skunk, you halfwit," Jamie says, but with hardly any venom; his mood is lighter.

Scott smiles. "He's got a point."

Preston raises an eyebrow but doesn't say anything, and the conversation continues around them. Scott looks over at Jamie, but he's engrossed in whatever Noel is saying.

Scott starts to wonder if he's fantasized about Jamie so much that maybe his mind went into overdrive and he created the entire kiss in his head. No, that's impossible. Scott might be a dreamer by nature, but this was too real to deny. He's *never* had a kiss that good; he couldn't have dreamt *that* kiss. Even his subconscious couldn't come up with something so life-changing, so perfect. But then why is Jamie so blasé about it? It obviously hasn't affected him in the same way. He's laughing at everyone's jokes and now he's standing up, waving at Adamo and telling Ashley to make sure Julia gets home in one piece.

"You're leaving?" Scott says.

"I have an early call time in the morning," Jamie says.

"I'll walk you out." Scott pushes his chair out and is halfway to standing when he feels Jamie's hand on his shoulder.

"No, it's fine. I called a cab," he says. "Stay… have fun." His voice is gentle, steady; he's the picture of composure. How is he so calm?

Scott's heart sinks at Jamie's reaction, but he sits back down anyway and looks forlornly up at him. This feels wrong. Scott wants to say something, but his mind is blank, and words won't come.

Jamie offers him a small smile and says, "Coffee Monday morning?"

Scott nods slowly and watches Jamie leave, his head spinning from both the alcohol and the confusion over Jamie's sudden nonchalance. He glances at Sheena to see her watching him suspiciously. He lifts his glass and takes a sip, smiling at her in what he hopes is a convincing way, though whether he's trying to convince himself or Sheena that he's fine, he isn't entirely sure.

Chapter 11

Jamie doesn't push Scott out of his life this time. In fact, everything is completely normal—almost too normal. Jamie texts Scott on Saturday to ask the name of the actor who played the love interest in the last movie they saw together. Scott replies—Tim Matheson—and Jamie says thanks. On Sunday, Jamie sends him a photo of a lamp: *Found this at a thrift store. Tacky or just quirky enough to work?* Scott replies: *If you paint it, I think it will be fine.*

Again, Scott is faced with the idea that he might have dreamt that kiss, because Jamie is definitely not acknowledging it. Maybe Jamie regrets it or, then again, maybe he wants Scott to bring it up first. Suspecting that one of those reasons is true, Scott decides to mention it when they meet for coffee on Monday. He'll lay it all out on the table, and, as much as it pains him, if Jamie still just wants to be friends, Scott will respect that. There's no need to make a bigger deal out of this than necessary.

But as much as Scott wants that to happen, he oversleeps Monday morning and has a crucial appointment with a printer. Jan West may be Price's biggest client, but she's not the only one, and Scott's been so busy with her campaign, he's been neglecting other projects.

Jamie is sitting at a table with two paper cups in front of him when Scott rushes through the door nearly twenty minutes late.

"Oh God, I'm so sorry," he says between rasping breaths. "I overslept and then I realized I had a nine a.m. meeting that I can't be late for. So I can't stay. Do you hate me? I hate me."

"Scott, it's fine," Jamie says, smiling. He hands Scott his coffee and says, "I got your coffee, so you're good to go."

Unfortunately, after that, things get busy for Scott; he's wrapping up everything for West's holiday campaign. So he and Jamie miss movie nights, and Tuesday lunches get pushed back further and further because Scott doesn't have as much free time as he would like. Work takes over his mind and his life; Jamie seems to take it in stride.

As time wears on, Scott feels as if he's missed his window of opportunity to talk to Jamie about the kiss. It's become an elephant in the room that neither of them mentions. So, when faced with the choice of bending to adapt to the situation at hand or breaking and upsetting the precious equilibrium of their friendship, Scott decides to bend.

Obviously Jamie regrets kissing him, and Scott doesn't want to bring it up if Jamie isn't ready. Besides, if Jamie does regret it and he's willing to move on, Scott is more than happy to comply.

When they finally get some time to hang out, Jamie invites Scott over to watch a movie. Usually they're at Scott's because Jamie's roommates are always around, but Julia and Ashley are going to be out, and Jamie insists that they spend the evening at his place.

"I'm so glad you wanted to do this," Scott says, pouring each of them a glass of wine. "I've missed our movie nights."

It's comforting that it's just the two of them again; Scott can't remember the last time they were alone for any length of time, and it's far less tense than he expected. There's no lingering awkwardness, and that itself should feel strange but doesn't.

"Me too," Jamie says. "We've both been so busy lately."

"I'm sorry about that," Scott says. "With the launch party coming up, I've been pulling twelve-hour days. Yvonne is ready to pull her hair out, and Lorelei's breathing down my neck to get that last shoot done. Did the agency contact you about that?"

"Yeah, they called this morning," he says. "Just me, huh?"

"Well, it's just the one suit and we'll be in the studio for it. When I saw it, I knew it would be perfect on you. Wait until you see Isaac's styling."

"I can't believe you didn't send me pictures," Jamie huffs. He's teasing; it feels good.

"I wanted to surprise you, silly. C'mon, let's go start this movie." Scott nudges Jamie's shoulder and picks up the two glasses. He follows Jamie into the living room.

As they're settling into the worn sofa, Jamie says, "You should be my date to the launch party." He looks down at the wine glass Scott hands him. "You know, since we both have to be there. Takes the pressure off of finding someone else."

"Right." Scott pauses, unsure if he wants to continue. This feels like a *moment*; he should say something. "Jamie, can I ask you a question?"

"As long as it's not 'What's your favorite season of *Project Runway*?' because you know I could never decide."

"No, it's not that, it's about that night at the club…"

Scott trails off when he sees Jamie tense, but he can't back out now. They need to talk about this—if for no other reason than to save his own sanity.

"It's just… I don't want there to be any question where we stand… Because we have coffee together, we do movie nights, lunch; we're friends, and this—" He gestures between them. "—is something really special to me, and I don't want to mess it up." He pauses for a deep breath. This is it. He's all in. "But then you kissed me, and it was so great—"

"It was?" Jamie interrupts.

"It was perfect, Jamie. *You're* perfect, and I just want us to—"

But he's cut off by the sound of the front door opening. He and Jamie both turn to look just as Ashley bounds in with two girls and a guy he's never seen before.

"Hey, guys," she says. "This is Angie and Jennifer, and Captain Ahab over there is called Rob."

She's balancing a pizza in her left hand and holding a case of beer with her right. "Jules texted me; she's headed home with her flavor of the week *and* her roommate. Told me to grab a couple of pizzas."

"I thought you were going out tonight."

"Change of plans," she says. "The restaurant was booked for a private party, and Rob didn't want to do sushi, so… pizza." She looks between Jamie and Scott and her eyes narrow. "I'm not interrupting anything, am I?"

"No!" Jamie practically shouts. "No, no… we're just watching a movie. The more the merrier, right, Scott?"

Scott swallows heavily. He'd just been about to confess his feelings. They were finally getting somewhere, but instead here they are, stuck in the middle of an impromptu house party with half a dozen strangers. Perfect.

"Right," he says. "The more the merrier." He takes a gulp of his wine and shivers as it burns down his throat.

* * *

Scott doesn't see Jamie until the photo shoot. He isn't himself and it shows in the photos.

"Jamie, can you try maybe angling your chin down more?" Zach asks. He snaps a few frames and looks at the preview on the screen, before turning to Scott. "How's that look from over there?"

Scott squints at the image on his laptop. "Something's not quite right," he says. "I can't put my finger on it." He stands up and walks over next to Zach. "Maybe the lighting?"

"I can try adding another strobe—make it harsher, maybe?"

"Yeah, let's try that," Scott says. "Jamie, take five."

Scott goes back to his laptop and scrolls through the last few shots. He can't quite figure out what's wrong with the photos. Everything is technically good, but Jamie's not connecting with the camera like he usually does. There's something missing from his eyes, as if his usual motivation is gone.

"Jamie, you got a sec?" he calls out.

Jamie looks up from his phone and nods, making his way over to Scott.

"What's up?" he asks.

"I was going to ask you the same thing. I'm just not seeing your usual … spark."

"I'm sorry," Jamie says, looking down at his folded hands. "I guess I'm just distracted. I'll try harder."

"Just try to relax," Scott says. "It's just me and Zach. You've done this a million times." He places a hand on Jamie's shoulder, trying to soothe him. He feels Jamie's muscles tense, so he drops his hand. "You ready?"

Jamie nods, and they get back to work. The lighting is better, making Jamie's angular features more severe; it should be working, but it's not. Zach's huffing a little, and Scott is losing his patience. He drops his head in his hand and considers the situation. He knows Jamie is off his game because of him; the unspoken things between them have become a weight neither of them is handling very well. It's his job to make sure Jamie's on his game, and he's failing, personally and professionally. They need to talk, but there's no time here on set.

Suddenly, Scott has an idea. "Hey, Zach," he says. "Mind if I try something?"

"I'll try anything at this point," he says.

"Okay, guys, just bear with me here."

Jamie looks up questioningly, but doesn't object.

Scott walks over to Zach and holds out his hand. "May I?"

Zach raises an eyebrow, but holds out the camera. Jamie's eyes light up with something new: a challenge, perhaps. Scott is transfixed, as if some force is holding him in place.

"Jamie, just make sure you maintain eye contact with the camera," Scott says. "Direct it all at the lens." What he means is: Take all that anger, desire, passion, frustration, whatever it is that is holding you back, whatever you're feeling, and channel it into your work. Let it go. He lowers his voice and leans in so only Jamie can hear him. "Direct it all at *me* if you have to."

Jamie nods, his eyes fixed on Scott's as his breathing picks up, and if it weren't for the camera and all the lights between them, Scott would swear they're back outside that bathroom, suspended in the second before Jamie kissed him. Then Jamie locks his gaze on the camera lens three feet from his face, determination apparent in the set of his jaw, and a hushed anticipation settles over them. Jamie blinks twice and relaxes into the posture that Scott instantly recognizes as his model's stance; he's ready to go.

Scott smiles and ducks behind the camera, using the viewfinder rather than the digital display. There's an intimacy in seeing Jamie through the focused view of the lens, and Scott is awestruck. It's like seeing Jamie for the first time, all of his emotions raw and his soul laid bare—and it's nothing like the pictures Scott used to get off to. This is Jamie the person, the one who is Scott's friend, not Jamie the model or the insane erotic fantasy that Scott had created around him. In that moment of realization, the shock of Jamie's beauty shoots through Scott like fireworks—a sharp point of light that erupts into a shower of sparks in his chest. He holds his breath and snaps the shutter. Zach had left it on a rapid-fire setting, so he shoots about ten frames at once, catching the subtle changes in Jamie's expression.

He glances down at the display; even at only three inches wide, he can tell the shots are what they're looking for. Scott lifts the camera back up and smiles. "All right, Jamie, let's try that again, and this time I want you to really take a risk. Try something new and don't hold back."

The set is eerily silent, only the click of the shutter and Jamie's subtle shifts in movement making any sound. Scott is certain Zach can hear his heartbeat; it's so loud in his own ears, there's no way it can't be heard from space—let alone five feet away— though he finds it hard to care because there's an energy in the room he's not felt before. And judging by the light in Jamie's eyes, Scott thinks that he also recognizes this groove they've somehow managed to get into.

Zach retreats behind Scott's laptop after a bit to see the photos as Scott shoots them.

"You look like you've done this before," Zach says, when Scott finally lowers the camera for a second to check a shot.

"Just as a hobby," Scott replies, without looking up. "In college."

Zach shrugs. "You're good," he says. "I'm impressed."

"Thanks," he says, before turning back to Jamie. "Okay. Give me *more*." He pauses, feeling as if they're on the verge of something, as if there's something lurking just under the surface and straining to get out. If he can only tap into it, find the right thing to say to pull just a bit more emotion out of Jamie. "I want to see whatever it is you're feeling … right now. Let it read on your face. It's just you and me."

Scott sees Jamie's jaw tense, just slightly, and his own breath catches. The hairs on the back of his neck stand up. Jamie grips his tie in his right hand and pulls it to the side, lifting up on his toes and tensing his whole body. As Scott clicks the shutter, he's overwhelmed with a flurry of emotions and pure visceral need. He wants to grab Jamie by that tie and take him to the back room and ravage him, pin him against a wall and kiss him until he begs for more. Jamie is visibly panting, and Scott wonders if he's thinking the same thing.

He never wants this feeling to end, this perfect connection— Scott, Jamie, and the camera—he wants to keep going, but he knows it has to end.

"I think we got it," Scott says finally. He tries to keep his face neutral, but his body is practically shaking with adrenalin.

"I'd say so," Zach says, fanning himself dramatically. "That was H-O-T hot."

Jamie seems frozen for a moment, almost as if the whole thing hasn't registered yet, and then he smiles, a beaming, all-over grin. "You really think so?"

"I think we got the best shots of the campaign today," Zach says. "Jamie, you were amazing!"

"Thanks," he says, blushing a little. "Scott helped. I mean—his direction. Channeling my emotions was a good suggestion." He scuffs his shoes on the concrete floor and looks up at Scott.

Scott meets Jamie's eyes and sees the same look Jamie had when he kissed him. His skin tingles with something new, something unexpected.

"Do you want to grab lunch?" Scott asks.

* * *

"God, you're breathtaking," Jamie says, standing in the doorway of Scott's bedroom. They'd stopped at his apartment so Scott could change his shirt, and they'd both been so distracted talking about the shoot, that Jamie had simply followed him in. Scott hadn't even realized he was there until he hears Jamie's voice behind him, and he freezes. Before turning around, he glances down at himself. He has his shirt off, and his pants are unbuttoned and slung low around his hips, a hint of the grey of his boxer-briefs peeking out of the fly.

Scott turns around slowly, unsure of what to do next.

Jamie's eyes flick down Scott's body before snapping back up to meet his eyes and widening in part shock, part arousal. "Did I say that out loud?" His voice is thin and raspy, as if he's having a hard time breathing.

Scott licks his lips and frowns slightly, his eyes narrowing. "Did you mean it?"

Jamie inhales and holds his breath, biting his bottom lip and then releasing it. "Yes?" The word comes out with his breath, and Scott crosses the room in an instant.

"Me too," he says. "When you kissed me, I—"

Jamie presses a finger to his lips, "Shh. No talking. Let's just…" and he trails off as he leans forward to brush his lips against Scott's, a tentative question that Scott answers by pushing forward into Jamie, rising up on his toes a little and rocking them both with the movement. Jamie catches him by his hips and steadies them both, holding Scott in place and drawing a groan from Scott's throat. He wants to be closer, so he opens his mouth to invite Jamie's tongue. It brushes against his, velvety and teasing, just a whisper of contact. Scott just wants this moment to last; he wants to savor it because it's so right.

This is where they should be; it's theirs.

But then Jamie's kissing becomes more insistent, more possessive, as he pulls his lips away and peppers Scott's face and neck with open-mouthed kisses.

"Jamie," Scott gasps. "I need you."

Jamie pauses, and pulls back to look at Scott, his eyes roving over Scott's face as if he's trying to decide something as he reads him like a book.

"You have me," he says finally. "However you want me."

That's all Scott needs to hear. He surges forward and grips Jamie by the waist, steering him toward the bed. When the back of Jamie's knees hit the edge, they're jolted a little, Scott's knees knocking against Jamie's shins as they fall in a tangle of limbs onto the sheets. Jamie's movements are frantic now, scrabbling for a place to hold onto Scott, but there's nothing to grab onto with him shirtless, so his hands paint Scott's skin with warmth, every sensation burning through him like fire.

Scott straddles Jamie and nudges his shirt up, trailing his palm along his smooth skin and feeling a prickle of stubble along his chest where the hair is starting to grow out from his most recent waxing.

"That tickles," Jamie says, shivering.

Scott pulls his hand back. "Sorry."

"No, it's fine," Jamie says, reaching for Scott's hand and placing it back on his torso. "I wasn't complaining."

Scott smiles down at him, and whispers "okay"—a tiny breath of a word that carries more weight than it should. Now that he has express permission to touch, Scott moves with intent, shoving Jamie's shirt farther up his chest so he can lower his head and rub his cheek along Jamie's ribs. The stutter and start of their dry skin ghosting over each other sends a shiver up his spine as goose bumps break out over his arms. Scott traces a loose figure eight over Jamie's side with his tongue and giggles when Jamie squirms beneath him.

After spending months memorizing every inch of Jamie's body on his computer screen, Scott delights in mapping out Jamie's dips and angles with his fingers and mouth, exploring in ways he's only dared to dream, as he undresses him and learns Jamie's rhythm. Scott treasures every caress and sigh, every shudder and gasp, unsure if he'll ever get the chance to do this again. Right now it doesn't matter, because he's here, and Jamie's here, and there's nowhere he'd rather be and nothing he'd rather do.

Jamie becomes gradually more vocal, his moans and high-pitched whimpering giving way to full-on groans and the occasional "oh God" or "Scott" until he's begging to be touched, to be released from the overwhelming surge of want coursing through them both. And Scott wants nothing more than to give it to him, to finally acquiesce to the pull of the tide washing over them. He reaches down between them and hooks his fingers under the waistband of Jamie's briefs, the only article of clothing separating Scott from the few inches of Jamie's skin he's only been able to fantasize about until now, as he follows the teasing strip of hair trailing down beneath his bellybutton and disappearing beneath tightly stretched cotton.

Scott, still in his own jeans, suddenly feels completely naked in front of Jamie. They've never been this real with each other before, and it's freeing and frightening in equal measure. The release he feels at just being able to touch, to explore… to *have*, is indescribable. He wants so much, but mostly he wants to savor.

Jamie raises up on his elbows at Scott's hesitance and lifts an eyebrow. "Everything okay?"

Scott nods eagerly. "You're just… *God*, Jamie, I can't stop looking at you."

"You've seen me before."

Scott shakes his head, even though Jamie's right, because it's just not the same. "Not like this," he says. "So open, and wanting, and…" he feels the corners of his mouth tug into a teasing grin. "So fuckable."

"So fuck me."

"What?"

"Fuck me," he says. "Have your way with me. Do what you've always wanted."

"Why do I feel like there's a catch?"

"No catch," Jamie says, trailing a hand along Scott's arm. It's feather light and teasing. "I want it too, Scott. Now stop talking and kiss me."

For a second Scott thinks he might stop them from crossing this line—his brain screaming "pull back, think, talk it through"—but his body, and the want of it all, is pulling him down and down and down, drowning him in Jamie, and he knows it's a losing battle to try to fight it any longer. There's no easing into it, no dip of the toe in the too-deep waters; he's diving forward headfirst, and the rush of it all feels like running through a sprinkler on a hot summer day, or pressing his face into the cool side of the pillow—fire-quenching and comforting all at once. It's all he can do to keep from telling Jamie he loves him.

So he looks down at Jamie and lets himself fall, losing himself in the feeling of Jamie's body pressed against his and the simple movements of their lips and tongues, tangled between them like vines. Everything else just slips away, and he's left with only the quiet desire for sex and its intimate release.

Once he decides to give himself over fully to the moment, Scott's thoughts turn unbridled; his fantasies run wild through his mind. He wants to take and taste and indulge. So he does.

Scott runs his right hand along Jamie's neck and pushes him back into the bed as Jamie arches his lower body into Scott's touch. His fingers thread through Jamie's hair, thick and glossy between them. He tugs experimentally, earning a small grunt of pleasure; he tugs harder and Jamie groans.

That one little sound is the first domino in a line, knocking down all of Scott's hesitation. It feels almost symbolic as he removes what remains of their clothing in quick, fluid movements, without pretense or delay.

And then it's groping and tasting and feeling and a thousand reasons they should have done this on the day they met. The sensations are heightened, every touch a point of light. Jamie's hands trace down Scott's back like flames licking at his skin and then he's squeezing Scott's ass and tugging him closer, rutting his hard cock against Scott's.

"God, Scott, please touch me," Jamie says. "I'm going to die if I don't come soon."

And without even thinking about it, Scott replies, "I want to suck you."

"Fuck yes, please." Jamie throws his head back and arches up, rutting against air, his hard cock bouncing freely as he searches for relief.

Scott makes his way down the bed until he's level with Jamie's flushed cock. Positioned between Jamie's legs, Scott realizes he's waited so long to be able to do this with Jamie that he doesn't even hesitate in wrapping his hand around the base and his lips around the head. He lowers himself slowly, though, wanting to feel Jamie fill his mouth.

He hears a choked-off moan above him, urging him on. He sucks harder and takes Jamie in as far as he can, the head of Jamie's cock just hitting the back of his throat. Jamie bucks up at the sensation, but Scott is just as quick, pulling back just enough to keep from choking.

"That feels so fucking good," Jamie says.

At the sound of Jamie's breathy declaration, Scott finds himself fighting the urge to rut down into the sheets. He needs to last, to make sure Jamie comes; it's his number one goal and he's going to make it happen. Scott just wants to see Jamie fall apart, to shout his name and tip over the edge into bliss—and all because Scott led him there.

It isn't long before Jamie is tensing up and Scott can feel his orgasm building. His balls draw up tight under Scott's fingertips and his thighs flex as Scott braces himself for the taste of Jamie's come in his mouth. But then Jamie's hand is on his shoulder and he's pushing against Scott, saying, "stop… stop."

Scott pulls off and looks up at him, flexing his jaw where it's begun to ache a little. "What's the matter?"

"If you don't stop I'm going to come," Jamie pants, an arm thrown over his face.

Scott smiles. "I thought that was the point."

"Oh, God, yes," Jamie sighs. "But I want us to both come, and I'm kind of a selfish prick. If you make me come, you're gonna be on your own. So…"

"I get the picture," Scott says biting back a laugh. "So what do you suggest?"

"Do you have condoms?" Jamie asks.

Scott looks at him for a moment, thinking, "I'm a single gay guy over the age of eighteen, what the fuck do you think?" before jumping up from the bed and digging around in his sock drawer for the box he knows is probably far more buried than it should be.

Scott turns around to face Jamie triumphantly, box of condoms and lube in his hand, and he's greeted with the most delicious sight: Jamie sprawled out spectacularly on display for him, chest flushed and heaving, his cock jutting up stiffly from between his legs as he crooks a finger at Scott to bring him back to the bed.

Stumbling and awkward, Scott makes his way back to the bed, and it has to be the most unsexy thing ever, but Jamie doesn't seem deterred as he grins at Scott before flipping himself over and arching his hips up seductively toward Scott.

Scott had hoped Jamie would remain on his back so he could see his face, but if this is how Jamie wants it, he'll happily comply. It briefly occurs to him that maybe Jamie hasn't had as much experience with sex as he'd first thought. Preston had said they fucked, and he knows what that often means when you're young: fucking for the sake of fucking and sticking to the positions where it's easiest to get off and best to avoid getting too attached.

It's the only time since Jamie came into his bedroom that he's considered their age difference. So if this is how Jamie wants it, Scott will give it to him. There's no point in forcing him out of his comfort zone if it's only going to scare him off again.

So he takes time to prepare Jamie, fairly certain he's not been having sex regularly, expertly using his fingers and lube to open him up.

"Jesus Christ, Scott," Jamie says, his voice muffled where his face is shoved into a pillow. "Will you just do it already?"

"I just… don't want to hurt you," Scott says, trying not to sound condescending. He doesn't want Jamie to think he's assuming anything.

Jamie turns his head to glare over his shoulder at Scott. "You're not going to fucking break me," he says. "I'm not some blushing virgin."

"Right… sorry."

Scott positions himself behind Jamie and lines up, hesitating only for a second before pushing forward into the tight heat of Jamie's body. Scott always likes this part the best, that moment when he can feel the other person's body yield to his own with an instant rush of pleasure and intimacy, as close as he can possibly be to another person. He groans, savoring the moment, but then Jamie is grinding back toward him and he forgets everything else.

It happens in a rush after that, having already worked themselves up so many times. Jamie is rutting into the mattress with each of Scott's thrusts as Scott grips tightly to his hips, meeting Jamie's rhythm as best he can. It's too much and it's probably going to be over far too soon, but Scott can't find it in him to care because it all feels so good.

Just as he thinks he can't hold on any longer, Jamie cries out, his body shuddering and clenching around him, and that's all Scott needs to send him over the edge too. The force of his own orgasm causes him to lose his balance, pressing his weight into Jamie. But Jamie doesn't seem to mind, sighing contentedly as Scott's body settles over him.

They lie like that for a moment, panting and coming down from the high of orgasm until Scott can feel his legs enough to lift up on his knees and pull out.

"Wow," Jamie breathes.

"That doesn't even begin to cover it," Scott replies, flopping down on the bed beside him.

"I'm glad we got that out of our systems," Jamie says matter-of-factly.

Scott looks over at him, wondering what he means. It definitely doesn't feel out of his system. He wants to do it all again… a lot. All the time. He laughs nervously and says, "Yeah… uh, me too." Scott hopes Jamie doesn't hear that questioning tone in his voice; he's not even sure why he agreed.

"Good," Jamie says, sitting up. He reaches to the floor for his underwear and stands to put them back on. He quickly finds all of his discarded clothing and turns back to Scott on the bed.

Scott is conflicted and suddenly very confused. Did Jamie really just think this was getting it out of his system? That they could go back to being friends after this? He tries to calm his breathing, not let it show, but he's almost panicking.

"It was stupid to try to deny that we're attracted to each other," Jamie says, still a little out of breath. He dresses quickly without looking at Scott. "But it was really starting to affect our work. Now we can focus again. It's a win-win." Jamie turns and smiles at him. "I'll call you," he says.

Scott props himself up on an elbow and opens his mouth to say something, anything to get Jamie to stay, but he freezes, the words caught in his throat. Instead, he nods and watches as Jamie walks out of his bedroom. When he hears the front door close, Scott drops his head back on the pillow.

Only moments before, he'd been so sure that he and Jamie were finally on the same page, but now everything's a mess and he feels used. How could he have been so blind? Jamie didn't want a relationship; it was just an attraction that they had ignored for far too long. The signs Scott thought he saw—the longing glances, the flirty banter, that kiss—all of it was nothing more than sexual tension, and he'd misread it as something more.

Well, if Jamie wants to go back to being friends, Scott can do that. He doesn't want to lose Jamie's friendship. He'll just have to figure out a way to live with his feelings and hope for the best.

Chapter 12

With the photo shoot wrapped, Scott doesn't have an excuse to see Jamie—not unless one of them initiates it. Everything feels stilted; their friendship is irrevocably changed. And then plans for coffee that week get canceled—Scott is too busy with work and needs to go in early—and a movie night gets postponed—Jamie books back-to-back jobs and his schedule changes. One thing after another gets in the way, and it just becomes easier to go with the flow.

It's not that Scott is avoiding Jamie; it's just that he doesn't know what to say. Clearly Jamie had wanted it to be a one-time thing, but Scott doesn't feel the same way. Or maybe he does. He's not really sure any more, and that's what's making it awkward. He thought he wanted a relationship with Jamie, but now, well, he wonders if maybe their age difference might be more problematic than he had realized. Even so, Scott knows he loves him, and that's the worst part.

So he avoids. He avoids and he tries to forget as he edits photos from the last day of the photo shoot. So far, he's not seeing any shots he likes; they're mostly the shots Zach had taken early in the day, and Jamie looks disconnected. He scrolls down until he finds the pose he's looking for: Jamie tugging on his tie and staring straight into the camera.

Everything about it makes a fire burn hot in his chest, with the memory of that day a bitter pill lodged in his throat. The absolute high of the photo shoot, Jamie naked and perfect on his bed, the punch to the gut when he'd left Scott lying there a wreck of emotion.

Scott suddenly hates the image; the burning passion in Jamie's eyes makes him want to delete it and forget it ever happened, but he can't bring himself to do that. It's still the most striking image of Jamie he's ever seen.

"Ooh, what's that?" Yvonne asks over his shoulder.

"Proofs for One West. I think this is *the* shot." He looks up at her expectantly.

"It's risky."

Scott nods. "Do you think Lorelei will go for it?"

"Maybe." Yvonne looks thoughtful. "We might as well try."

"What do *you* think?" Scott asks, hoping she agrees with him. This is the image he wants to build the entire campaign around, and things might go a little more smoothly with her support.

"Honestly?" she asks. "It's a fucking amazing shot and if you don't fight tooth and nail to keep it, I will personally fire you."

* * *

"It's just too much of a risk, Scott," Lorelei says after Scott finishes his presentation. "Jan is going to want another option."

"I don't want to give her options," he says. "I believe in this campaign. It's the right one. I'm sure of it."

"It's definitely eye-catching," Lorelei says, "but you've got to look at this from my perspective. I'm trying to run a business here, and I need happy clients. Jan West is picky, and that's putting it mildly. I can't risk putting her off and possibly nixing the spring campaign."

"She won't."

Lorelei looks down at the folder in front of her where Scott has assembled a brief. She flips through a few pages, biting her lip as she twirls a pen between her fingers. Without looking up, she asks, "Are you one hundred percent sure about this?"

"Absolutely."

She looks up at him. "Willing to bet your job on it?"

Scott swallows and takes a deep breath. Is he that sure? There is the off chance his judgment has been clouded by his feelings for Jamie, but then he remembers Yvonne's reaction and the way everyone else had absolutely fallen in love with the photos and designs. Lorelei's the only holdout before they go to the client.

Of course, the dark horse in all this is Jamie. He's four inches too short, and a completely different type of model than Jan has ever used as the face of her line, which, if he's honest about it, is *why* Yvonne had cast him in the first place. They both knew the job needed something fresh. It's the best campaign Price has ever done. Scott smiles as he thinks of what this kind of exposure could mean for Jamie. That thought tips the scale.

"You know what, Lorelei? I've never been more sure of anything in my life."

* * *

Scott's phone rings just as he steps out of the meeting. It's Jamie. Despite all the anger and hurt, he can't help but be excited to tell Jamie about the campaign.

"Hey," he says. "Perfect timing. I have great news. I just met with Lorelei and she green-lighted the campaign. You're going to be the new face of One West."

"Oh wow… really?!" Jamie's excitement is palpable even over the phone. "Oh my God, Scott, that's fantastic!"

"We still have to run it by Jan, but I know she's going to love it. Congratulations!"

"Oh my God."

Scott laughs. He's shocked and excited Jamie, and he's giddy with it. "So, I was thinking for the launch party…"

"Oh," Jamie says, his excited tone fading in an instant. "Actually that's why I'm calling. I uh… well, there's no easy way to put this. I can't go with you… as your date."

Scott is speechless. He knows their friendship had been awkward lately, but he didn't think Jamie was angry with him. Maybe their one slip-up affected Jamie more than he had thought.

"Is this about what happened between us?" Scott says, lowering his voice so he won't be overheard in the busy office.

"No, no," Jamie says, his voice pitching higher and taking on a breathy quality. "Um, I just forgot I already had a date." Scott can hear Jamie's breathing; it's uneven and heavy. "I'm really sorry." The apology sounds tacked on, an afterthought.

"Why do you keep pushing me away?" Scott asks, stepping into an empty conference room and closing the door.

"I'm not pushing you away, Scott. I told you. I have a date with someone else."

Jamie sounds frustrated, but Scott doesn't care. Jamie's words have hit a nerve that was already raw, and he wants answers.

"Then why do I feel like this is some sort of test, Jamie? It's like, ever since we met, all I do is jump through hoops for you, and every time I think I've jumped through them all, you put another one up in front of me."

"Scott…" Jamie pleads. "It's not like that. I promise."

Jamie's words practically go unheard. Scott is so angry he can barely think. "It's *exactly* like that, Jamie. Every time I think we're getting somewhere, you push me away, and there's only so much I can take. I'm sick of being treated like your enemy. We're supposed to be friends."

"Well then maybe we shouldn't *be* friends anymore," Jamie says.

"See? That's exactly what I'm talking about. Things get a little dicey and you act like a fucking child!"

"Fuck you, Scott."

"No, I'm pretty sure I fucked you."

He knows that's a low blow, and he waits for Jamie to return the volley. Scott looks down at his phone and sees that Jamie disconnected the call. He hung up. Scott grips his phone as tight as he can to keep himself from flinging it across the room.

* * *

As it turns out, Jan West loves the entire campaign. She's so excited about it, in fact, that she expands the launch party and moves it up a week. Scott barely has time to think about his fight with

Jamie, but it consumes him nonetheless. If it weren't for Yvonne and a team of amazing event planners, he'd be totally screwed.

But the night of the launch party finds Scott curled up on his sofa watching *When Harry Met Sally* and trying desperately not to think about Jamie. Of course, it's a completely pointless task because it's all he can think about. He wants to be at that party with Jamie, watching him bask in the glow of his own success, proud to be with Scott and proud of the work they've done together. He wants to be able to enjoy this accomplishment—the ad campaign looks flawless and everyone is already talking about the new line, and most especially Jamie—but Scott can't bear to look at Jamie and not be with him. Plus, it's not fair to Jamie for Scott to be a distraction at such an important moment. So instead he's sitting at home, wallowing in his own misery, powering his way through a bag of individually wrapped chocolates.

"What are you doing home?" The door slams shut behind Ben as he turns on the lights. "And in the dark?"

Scott sighs and drops his head back on the sofa. It's immature of him to avoid the party, but the idea of being there and watching Jamie on the arm of another guy is too much. He'd told Yvonne he was sick and he needed her to cover for him. She had looked as though she didn't believe him for a second, but she didn't question him. She simply took the reins and told Scott she hoped he felt better soon.

Scott grabs another piece of chocolate from the open bag on the coffee table, and studies the blue foil wrapping for a moment. "Jamie bailed on me, and I didn't feel like going alone."

He's such a coward, and worse still, a coward sitting at home alone eating junk food while watching a romantic comedy about friends who become lovers. It's torture.

"He's not still upset about the blow job thing, is he?" Ben asks, sitting down next to him on the sofa.

"No, he said he forgot he already had a date, and thanks for that by the way."

"I said I was sorry," Ben says. "But I call bullshit on that excuse. I think he chickened out."

"Maybe," Scott says absently as he turns his attention back to the TV. He unwraps the piece of chocolate still in his hands and pops it in his mouth. He's just about to throw the wrapper on the coffee table when he sees the message printed on it: *Don't be afraid to go after what you want.* The same message is printed on the crumpled wrapper he'd saved from a discarded box of Jacob memories. The only thing he'd saved because he didn't want to forget. He stares at it for a moment, wondering if he believes in fate.

"*I'm* the chicken," Scott says, looking up at Ben.

"I think the appropriate response here is *duh*," Ben says with a look of smug satisfaction. He adds more kindly, "So, what are you going to do about it?"

Scott pinches his fingers against the bridge of his nose; a dull headache is beginning to form behind his eyes. He glances from the wrapper still in his hands to the TV and back again. Harry is in the midst of having his epiphany about Sally and it suddenly occurs to him: This is them—him and Jamie, and he's sitting at home feeling sorry for himself when he should be at that party telling Jamie how he feels. Because the truth is, he's in love with Jamie, has been since that first night they had drinks together and he finally saw him as a person instead of an image on a screen. And yet he'd insisted they were only friends at every turn, trying to shield himself from the lingering specter of rejection.

Suddenly, none of that matters.

"I gotta go," he says suddenly, to himself more than Ben.

He jumps up and throws his blanket to the floor, making a beeline for his bedroom to change his clothes. He begins searching for any clean shirt in his closet that looks formal enough to get him in the door at the launch party. As he swipes at hangers frantically, he spies the vest he wore to that first photo shoot when he'd desperately wanted to impress Jamie. It's hanging there mocking him with the knowledge of how badly this could all backfire. Determined to at least tell Jamie how he feels, he pushes it to the left, and his eyes fall on the T-shirt Jamie had given him in honor of his promotion. He shakes his head and laughs at himself. If he believed in fate, he would definitely see this as a sign. The next shirt on the rack is clean and has buttons. Scott declares it a winner and throws it on. He's dressed and out the door in less than five minutes. A light rain has begun to fall, but he doesn't want to go back upstairs for an umbrella.

He practically runs the whole way, not even considering grabbing a cab, even as his lungs begin to burn. When he finally is too out of breath to run, he walks. Unfortunately, walking gives him time to think. All those weeks of denial, the time lost, the hurt feelings, that confusing kiss—all of that could have been avoided if he'd just been able to face his feelings and tell Jamie he loved him. Even after Jamie had left his apartment staunchly proclaiming the attraction was now "out of their systems," he should have said something.

He starts rehearsing what he's going to say.

"Jamie, I've been so stupid."

"Jamie, I'm so sorry."

"Jamie, I'm in love with you."

Scott breaks into a run again, ignoring the dull ache beginning to form in his lower back as he starts checking street signs to make sure he's headed in the right direction. His breath is coming out in short bursts that can be seen in the frigid November air, but he doesn't slow down.

When he finally arrives, the party is in full swing. People are dancing, laughing, having a good time. Posters from the campaign are everywhere—dozens of larger-than-life Jamies surrounding Scott and daring him to fail. But he shakes it off. He isn't going to fail; he knows it in his bones, because suddenly he can picture his future with Jamie. Beach vacations and a shared apartment, a dog, alternating Christmases between St. Louis and Chicago, everything he'd been too scared to ask of anyone—it's all crystal clear now, the future that will become their backstory. It's what he wants, and it's everything.

Desperate to find Jamie, Scott ducks between party-goers, dodging waiters and their trays of champagne, but there's still no sign of him. He spots Yvonne, who looks shocked when she sees Scott weaving through the crowd. Offering a smile but no explanation, he turns away from her and starts scanning the room again. Finally, he spots a familiar head of over-styled hair atop a tall, lanky frame. He's leaning against the bar and flirting with the bartender.

"Preston, have you seen Jamie?" Scott asks, his eyes still roving frantically about the room.

Preston looks as if he's ready to tease for a moment, but something in Scott's frazzled appearance must tell him now's not the time, because he answers quickly.

"He just left," Preston says. "Said he had a date he was late for…"

"Oh," Scott says. He's sure the disappointment is plain as day on his face, but he doesn't care. Let Preston and everyone else think what they want. It doesn't matter anymore. "Thanks."

So that's it. He's too late. Jamie is already interested in someone else, and he blew it. He fucking blew it.

Scott heads home feeling defeated and quite stupid for thinking Jamie would be interested in more than just friendship. The sky opens up as he steps outside, and he curses himself for leaving his umbrella at home.

The rain quickly soaks through Scott's thin cotton shirt, and the peach fabric drapes over him like a translucent second skin. He tugs at it, trying to get some relief from the weight of the shirt pressed against his chest, but it's no use. He's soaked clean through. As he enters his building, he's already unbuttoning it and imagining the blessed relief of stepping into a hot shower. He runs a hand through his hair to get it out of his eyes before reaching into his pocket for his keys. When he looks up, he sees Jamie, standing across from his apartment door, hands in his pockets and an unidentifiable look on his face.

"You're here," Scott says, as his mind races to figure out why Jamie is standing in his hallway. Why isn't he on his date? Why hadn't Ben let him in? "Why are you here?" he asks finally.

"I wanted to see you."

"But Preston said—"

Jamie's eyebrows shoot up. "You went to the party?" he asks.

"To find you."

Jamie steps closer, his eyes searching Scott's face. "Why?"

Scott doesn't answer, instead asking a question of his own. "Preston said you had a date?"

Jamie smiles and glances down at his own feet. A puddle is forming between them where Scott is dripping. "No, I told him I was late for one. About four months late."

Scott shivers; whether it's from being cold and wet or from Jamie's words, he's not sure. "Jamie, what are you saying?

"What I'm saying is, I'd like to go on a date with you, and I'm sick of trying to pretend that we're just friends."

"Jamie…"

"Let me finish," he pleads.

"Okay."

"I know I was the one who said just friends, but it's only because I was so afraid. I haven't been very lucky with relationships, and I keep people at arm's length because of it, but you saw through all that. Even when I tried to push you away, you wouldn't let me, and you're… well, *you*." He reaches up to cup Scott's face with his hand and strokes his cheek with his thumb. "You're this ridiculous dork with tattoos who wears neck ties and cardigans just as often as he wears graphic T-shirts and cargo shorts. You sing along to musicals and drink disgusting drip coffee with too much sugar, and you let me have my way even when it's not what you want. And I may only be nineteen, Scott, but I know what I want. And I want you. That is, if you'll have me."

Scott isn't sure what to say, which overture to respond to first, because his hands are shaking and his heart is racing and Jamie is staring at him with so much hope in his vibrant green eyes that it's dizzying. Jamie wants him, and it's not a dream—though he considers pinching himself to be sure.

"Well, say something," Jamie says finally.

Scott opens his mouth to speak, but then he realizes words aren't necessary. Jamie's said it all. He inches forward and rises up on his toes just enough so his face is level with Jamie's. He smiles, and kisses him. A soft, sweet, barely there kiss. He's not trying to prove anything, so there's no urgency; he's simply making a promise.

Jamie pulls back from the kiss, resting his forehead on Scott's.

"And all this time I thought you weren't interested," he says, his smile plain in his tone.

"*Me*?" Scott says, finally opening his eyes. "You kept saying you just wanted to be friends. It was killing me not being able to tell you how I felt."

Jamie's expression turns serious. "I'm sorry it took us so long to get here," he says.

"Don't be," Scott says. "It was worth the wait." He pauses before smiling at Jamie and adding, "And the one-night stand."

When Jamie laughs, it tickles his nose. Scott leans back just enough to focus on Jamie's entire face. "You have freckles," Scott says with wide eyes and a warm smile. He grazes his fingers over Jamie's forehead and nose, plotting them out like pinpoints on a map.

"Yeah," Jamie says, looking self-conscious about it as he tries to put a hand up over his face.

Scott pulls his hand out of the way and kisses the tip of his nose.

"I can't believe I never noticed that before. I've spent months staring at your face—your body—all day long, and I never noticed. How could I miss that?" His voice is low and soft, an intimate whisper of precious words.

"Good makeup artist, I guess," Jamie teases, a light blush making some of his freckles more prominent than before and obscuring others.

"No, I like this better," Scott says, his eyes searching Jamie's face as if he's trying to memorize it. "I can see *you*. The parts you never show anyone else."

"It's still me," Jamie says, ducking his head.

Scott places a finger under his chin and tilts his head up. Jamie's eyes meet his and it's as if the world is laid at his feet. He's never seen anything so beautiful in his life.

"Yes, and I love you," Scott says.

Jamie's eyes light up. "You do?"

Scott nods and kisses him again, feather-light and affectionate.

"Even when I'm bitchy and jealous?" Jamie teases

"Especially then," Scott says, looping his hands tight and low around Jamie's waist. "We might never have become friends if you hadn't been such a bitch that first day."

"Well someone's eyes were bugging out of his head and he was acting like a complete weirdo."

"I couldn't help it," Scott says. "This incredibly sexy man had just walked into my life, and I didn't know what to do."

Jamie rolls his eyes, but it's playful. Then his expression turns serious.

"I love you too, you know," he says.

Scott smiles because those are the best words he's ever heard. Music to his ears. He feels giddy and silly and ready to burst.

"Good to know," he says. "Otherwise it would be pretty forward of me to ask you to come inside on our first date."

Acknowledgments

I owe my unending gratitude to everyone at Interlude Press—Lex Huffman, CL Miller, Annie Harper and my fellow authors—this book would literally not exist if it weren't for you. To Mimsy Hale for not loving everything I write but reading it anyway. To Brian Brewer for being a dear friend and snarky, opinionated reader. To Becky Shepherd, my favorite graphic designer, for inspiring this story in the first place and then designing the sexy cover art for it.

I'd also like to thank my mother for always encouraging me to read… well, except for that one time she ripped a book out of my hands so I'd just clean my room already. I'd also like to thank her for being a "mean mom." It paid off, I promise.

Thank you to anyone who has ever encouraged me or has been willing to listen to me ramble on endlessly about characters, plots and butts—especially Ryan, Knits, Lissa, Mav and all of my Tumblr family and fic readers. You helped make this happen.

And to my husband, Josh, thank you for accompanying me on this crazy journey called life and, most importantly, for letting me pursue my dreams. Think it'll work?

interlude **press**

A Reader's Guide to *Designs On You*

Questions for Discussion

1. Scott "designs" a persona for Jamie as he works on the ad campaign. How does Jamie manipulate his own image for different audiences and individuals?

2. How does technology influence our perception of strangers, and how does that affect the development of Scott and Jamie's relationship?

3. What is the role of voyeurism in a celebrity-driven culture? Is our fascination with celebrity based on simple curiosity, or fantasy?

4. How did Scott and Jamie's past relationships shape their early interaction?

5. What are the roles of fantasy versus reality in *Designs On You*, and how do they play out?

interlude **press**

One Story Can Change Everything.

interludepress.com

Twitter: @interludepress   * * *   Facebook: Interlude Press
Google+: +interludepress   * * *   Pinterest: interludepress
Instagram: InterludePress